LIFE ON PAUSE

LUCIA POPELASOVA

Copyright © 2023 **Lucia Popelasova**

All rights reserved. No part of this publication may be reproduced, distributed, or transmitted in any form or by any means, including photocopying, recording, or other electronic or mechanical methods, without the prior written permission of the publisher, except in the case of brief quotations embodied in critical reviews and certain other noncommercial uses permitted by copyright law. For permission requests, write to the publisher, addressed "Attention: Book Rights and Permission," at the address below.

Published in the United States of America

ISBN 978-1-962569-44-6 (SC)
ISBN 978-1-962569-42-2 (HC)
ISBN 978-1-962569-43-9 (Ebook)

Lucia Popelasova
222 West 6th Street
Suite 400, San Pedro, CA, 90731
luciaso@yahoo.com

Order Information and Rights Permission:

Quantity sales. Special discounts might be available on quantity purchases by corporations, associations, and others. For details, contact the publisher at the address above.

For Book Rights Adaptation and other Rights Permission. Call us at toll-free 1-888-945-8513 or send us an email at admin@stellarliterary.com.

For my dearest son, sunshine Kevin

Thank you for all your love and patience with my mistakes and appreciation for my everyday effort to do it all better. No sacrifice was ever big enough to have the honor to be a mommy to a unique person like you.

"If you look hard enough, you can always find the bright side."

♥

ACKNOWLEDGMENTS

With love and many thanks to all; without, I won't be me.

My son Kevin (It's the best no matter what to give you a hug or get the one from you to get the will to move forward while knowing we are trying our best.); my parents and brother (I'm still learning how you had the courage to let me on my own find the place in the world while keeping your love and safety net around me.); Aunt Hanka (My head is up, and I'm going forward.); and the rest of the family, true friends, and many great people that entered some way in my life: Katie (My dear "mother hen", thank you for not letting me fall too down!); Pavel (Thank you for our talks about life, projects and for supporting me by actions to make me believe there's so much to live for.); Mirka (You know your truth…); Lucka, Hanka (Glad we still have hope and faith.); Miska (Thank you for many things that showed you care.); Claudia (I guess we should stop looking for better year to start but make today the better one.); Adelka (We are far away, but you are in my thoughts as much as possible as a true friend that I'm sorry to missed so much out of your life); Sandra (No one should walk over anybody.); Genya (Through that "whatever", I thought of you, and I knew it'll be me "keep going".); Greg (I'll always remember: "Lucia, you can do it."); Teresa (It'll be nice to enjoy tea with you, but both of us will be probably managing million other things while doing so.); Suhail (Thank you once more for giving me the last needful push to get focused to finished this book by telling me to make time!); J.W.

(We are the only ones walking in our shoes; no one else can do it… They can try, but that's not the same.); Linda (Hope you'll enjoy this book.); Ludka, Stano (Thank you for the kindness and closest reminder of family I came from.); Valerie, Lonnie (There was never doubt that you're here for us!); Matt (Doesn't matter if we named goal or project till we will put our best effort to it to make it reality.). I can keep writing, but instead, I'll make space for the book to be enjoyed; and to others, I'll talk to in person.

Without you all, it won't be me. So thank you for you all as well as for any extra hours in the day or nighttime I did make it for paper and pen with music on.

"Whatever we think is possible will determine our reality. Impossibilities are possible."

Chapter 1

With the mind in the time few days back, sitting on one of the Florida's beaches, resting on each other by touching shoulders, happily enjoying the look at the sunrise with hot coffee and bare feet feeling still cold sand, he could almost smell the aroma of coffee in their mugs and Elli's scent. His face lit up with a smile until he felt a sudden sharp pain. His right hand automatically touched the spot across his chest.

"Elli, sweetheart, hi. I'm going to take the work home. Sorry for canceling our lunch which I was very excited for. I don't feel very well, honey. But I'm just probably tired. Don't worry about me, and I hope you can still enjoy the lunchtime with Lisa. I will see you at home later on."

Elli and Lisa were coworkers who enjoyed each other's company even outside of the office.

"Lisa! Wait! Any plans for lunchtime? Danny just cancelled on me," said Elli.

"Not really! Today I was supposed to catch up on some work, but hey, we can go outside and split. I have enough for both of us. The work will not run away. Unfortunately," Lisa said and winked at Elli.

Both laughed and stepped out of the office building to enjoy their lunchtime on very warm September day in Chicago.

"So how were things in Florida? Sorry, we didn't really have the time to talk about that. Everything seems to be so hectic lately."

"It does! It was great! I can't say a one single bad word about it."

"You are glowing, girl. What did Danny do with you there?"

"I know! I'm just so happy, Lisa. It was all so simple. We didn't do anything fancy. We went to the beach, talk, dine, cook. You know."

"Yeah, yeah. I know. All what I didn't do in last one hundred years," said Lisa, and both of them smiled at each other.

"Danny sure do have great ideas. This was so unexpected. And last morning there, he woke me up before sun."

"So you guys went to see the sunrise or?"

"Lisa! Silly. Yes. Sunrise."

"Cool. I'm jealous!"

After talking and eating for a while, Elli nervously checked her watch. She felt kind of silly to be thinking about Danny, but she couldn't help.

"Will that bother you too much if I'll call to Danny?"

"Don't be silly. Of course not! Aren't you going to see him after work? Hey, I'm just teasing you!"

Both burst into laughter again. They always had a good time together, even when the day at work didn't go smooth. Each of them was so different. Lisa was so spontaneous; Elli was all for planning.

"What is it, Elli?"

"I don't know. It's just that feeling. He is not picking up the phone."

"Why do you worry?"

"It's not like him at all. He never did that."

"Didn't you say he went home because he didn't feel very well?"

"Yes, but—"

"But what, Elli? He's probably taking a nap right now. That's why he is not responding, or he is in the bathroom. Or I'm sure there are many other or…"

"I guess."

"You're so cute."

"It's just that feeling. I wish I can leave right now. But I still need to place some more orders which I can't leave for tomorrow."

"Then we better go back to work!" said Lisa while picking up all the lunch pieces.

Elli was staring at the clock while she was placing the orders. It felt like one minute is taking forever to pass.

"You are still here?" asked Lisa when she was passing Elli's desk. "Do you want me to finish up something for you so you can go?"

"No, thanks, Lisa. Now I just need to make one phone call to make sure all info in papers is correct, and I'm wrapping up for today before anything else will pop up!"

"Okay. Hope Danny will feel better! Let me know!"

"Thanks, Lisa. I will."

Elli was hoping not to get stuck in the traffic. She thought that if she'll just get on the road now, she'll fit between lunch and first work, ending wave of traffic. Her car was really heated up from the sun. Her rushing to the car didn't help. She was already sweaty by the time she reached for burning handle of the car door. She rolled down the windows to get the air moving through her fine reddish hair that was now framing her face. Elli tried to call Danny again but without any answer. She pushed the pedals down like she could push the time. Looking at their apartment building brought huge relief to her body. It made her smile shortly to herself by the memory of them walking on the beach few days ago and making the plans to move after winter to their own place. They just needed to decide on the place—if they wanted to be closer to the Chicago downtown or the suburbs. Both of the options were the winning options to them. And now she felt so good and happy to see this building, with small balconies where they were able to fit the seats and little table with few plants around.

Elli parked the car and took her stuff in hurry and ran toward the building entrance. She didn't want to wait for an elevator, so she ran upstairs to their third floor. With shaking hand and heavy breathing, she opened the door.

"Danny! Danny, where are you?"

The apartment gave her just silent answer back. She walked through their living room straight toward the bedroom where she quietly approached Danny's side of the bed. He looked so peaceful. Asleep.

"Danny. Honey. I'm back home," Elli said softly, almost whispering while she put her hand on his hair. She loved to touch his hair, usually standing in every possible direction.

"Danny? Danny!" Elli realized she didn't feel him breathing. She panicked. She started to shake his body and repeated his name over and over again. But the silence was only interrupted by her crying voice. With one hand, she wiped her hair off her face, while with the other, she wiped the tears off her eyes.

"I have to stop. I need to put myself together. This won't help him."

She started to work on CPR. No change. After a while when she couldn't feel the strength anymore in her hands, she ran as fast as she could to her purse.

"Where is it? That's insane! Always in my hand. Now when I need it, I can't find that stupid phone!" She shook all out of her purse on the floor. "There it was!" She got it out as the last one.

"Hello, emergency? I need help!"

Elli kept trying to get him back. She wanted so badly to hear him breathing, to see him open his eyes, and to look at her and say, "Sorry, sweetheart. I didn't hear you come. How was your day? How was the lunchtime without me?"

The emergency team arrived. They made her to step aside. She stood there trying her best to answer all the questions about Danny while watching them do their work. Her heart was beating so fast she barely could hear a thing. All she could feel were her own tears running down the cheeks.

Few people got slowly out of the room when she realized somebody's voice said the cruel words aloud: "Madame, I'm very sorry. There was nothing else we could do."

She felt like in the bad movie scene. She could almost hear herself screaming, "No, don't go! You need to help him! He said, he said he just don't feel very well. He needs you. I need you. I need Danny back by me."

"Madame. Madame, are you okay?" said one of the paramedics while supporting her to stand up and trying to move her to the other room to sit.

"We can get you something to feel better."

She looked at him with eyes filled up with tears and asked one question, "Can you get my Danny back?"

"Sorry, madame, we tried our best."

"Then there is nothing that you can do for me to feel better."

After that, she didn't really hear what they were saying. She just found herself doing automatically what she was asked to do. Everybody left. The place was filled with silence.

Elli could hear the hand of the clock movements, breaks squeaking from the near street, noises of the elevator loading up with some of the neighbors, and her thoughts. They were changing so fast that they made her suddenly so dizzy. She felt sad and mad. So helpless. Her right hand hit the wall and slowly slid down on it while she put her forehead on it with all the weight of her body and her thoughts. It felt cool and soothing. Then she turned around and put all the weight of her back and shoulders against it and slowly let her body slide down. She wrapped her folded knees and broke into tears.

The sun was long gone when she stopped. Her Danny was gone too, and there was no way to change it.

Chapter 2

"Elli, wait!" called Lisa while running few feet behind her. Both wrapped up in heavy sweaters.

"Hi."

"Hi."

"Wow, that October weather is something! Few days ago, we were enjoying sunny lunchtime together and today! I'm sorry, Elli, I didn't mean to …" Lisa suddenly stopped remembering the sunny lunchtime on the day when Danny died.

"It's okay, Lisa," said Elli with tears filling up her eyes again.

"Oh, come here!" Lisa hugged Elli as tight as she could.

"You are doing so great! Look at you, my brave girl." Both stood there lost in a moment.

"Why, Lisa? Why? I still don't understand. It's so cruel. Why Danny? Why now? We were so happy. We have made so many plans. He … I miss him so much! It's even hard to breathe when I'm thinking about him. I'm always waiting for his question to come when I wake up—'What do you feel like to have for breakfast?' Or if that tie goes well with the rest of his outfit. Or how was my day. Or—" Elli broke down into tears. "But nothing.

Just that silence is real!"

"Elli, please, come to my place. At least for few days."

"No, Lisa. I can't."

"Of course you can!"

"You don't understand! I can't! At our place, I can still see him. I can still feel him. I'm afraid if I'll be more than my work time away, he won't be there anymore."

"Elli, do you feel okay? You look so pale. Let's go inside. You are shaking."

They stepped into the nicely heated-up building with smell of morning coffee in the air. Elli collapsed her body on the chair at her desk, while Lisa brought two freshly brewed cups of coffee. "Enjoy. That should get you color back," said Lisa while handing still steamy cup of coffee to Elli. She already started sipping on her own.

Elli automatically raised the cup of coffee close to her lips. Once the strong aroma of it hit her nostrils, she put the cup down and ran to the restroom. She returned to her desk more pale than before. Lisa handed to her coffee cup.

"Boy, you really don't look good."

"I think a cup of tea will be better," Elli said to Lisa and tried her best to put a smile on her face. She didn't want her to be worried about her. She knew how much support she had in her, but that was not what she was longing for. Each morning, she forced herself to set up something for herself for breakfast while she kept Danny's favorite mug on the table. By looking at it, she felt better. Like in any moment, he'll appear in the kitchen by their little table always covered with nice tablecloth, and he will reach for it. Realizing the reality, she had to force herself to hold the tears back.

At the evenings, she found one of Danny's shirts, and it brought her comfort. It felt like she was wrapped in his arms. Lately, it was difficult to find the position to fall asleep in. Well, lately, nothing seemed to work out for Elli.

"Elli! Elli! Hello! I'm here. Where are you?" Lisa was holding Elli's tea in one hand. Meanwhile, she was waving with the other in front of Elli's face.

"Oh, I'm sorry, Lisa," said Elli while taking a hot cup of tea from Lisa.

"Be careful. It's still hot. Hope you'll drink it up while it's hot. It's more relaxing this way. Are you sure you don't need anything else? Did you eat?"

"Me and my tea. I'll be fine. Thank you, Lisa, for everything."

"Okay," said Lisa while checking up Elli by looking over the edge of her cup. She noticed Elli's shaking hands and very pale face.

"If you need anything, you know where I'm."

"I know. Thank you."

They both exchanged short smile and got to the work. Things were keeping them busy through the rest of their workday. The weather kept them in for a lunchtime since rain was pouring for hours. The sky was showing no sign for any changes to a better sunny weather.

"I'm beat up!" said Lisa while crushing herself onto the edge of Elli's desk.

"What are you doing tomorrow?" It was Friday before longer weekend. Lisa was already having some plans with her new boyfriend, but she felt like she should be here for Elli.

"Well, not much. I was thinking some grocery shopping, laundry, maybe taking a bike ride which I haven't used since ..." Elli broke into silence. "Which I haven't used for a while."

It was Danny who introduced her to the biking. He was natural in any physical activity. For Elli was so easy and joyful to follow him. She loved to watch him with how much focus and passion he was doing all. Elli shook her head, pretending to get rid of the hair in her eyes, but with all her mind, she was trying to keep away tears.

"Okay. That sounds pretty exciting," Lisa said and smiled. "What do you say? You and me. Friday after work movie. If you don't feel like going to theater, we'll watch something at yours or at my place. Ice cream, reading magazines, books, boat riding, or we can go for horseback riding?"

"Sounds good. Didn't you have already plans with 'Mr. Last One'?"

"Yes, but it's nothing, that can wait."

"Lisa, I don't want to ruin anything for you!"

"Elli, there were so many I put first. Listen, if it's supposed to work, it'll even when I'll spend some time with my great friend!"

"Are you sure?"

"Of course I am. Don't even think about it! So at my place?"

"Can we be at mine?"

"Okay, no problem! So see you tomorrow. After work, I'll be all yours with big luggage."

"So, Elli, are you ready?"

"Ready for what?"

"Elli, come on! Don't tell me you forgot about our weekend!"

At that moment, Lisa raised up in the air huge bag. "Because I'm ready." And she put on a big smile.

"You are not planning to move in?"

"No worries. I'm still enjoying my freedom."

"All right then, let's go. I'm ready."

They only took Elli's car and left Lisa's in the garage at work. The air did smell good after yesterday's rain. Elli was driving the car with windows rolled all the way down. Both of them enjoyed the cool breeze touching their faces and messing up their hair by lifting it up and, after some twists, dropping down suddenly—repeating all over again. The music from the radio station was so loud that none of them was trying to start any conversation at that time. Lisa was very happy to see Elli relaxed, and one time, she caught her singing her lungs out.

"Okay. We're here," said Elli while parking the car by her apartment building. "What did you pack in there?" asked Elli while pointing at Lisa's bag. "It really looks like a lot. For one overnight."

"I know, but all looked like it's the most important thing. Where are you going?"

"Stairs."

"Hello, are you nuts? Look at this!" Lisa lifted her stuff up in the air.

"I'll meet you upstairs," Elli said and giggled.

"Come on, Elli. Keep me company."

"Okay," Elli said and turned from walking toward the staircase to getting back to Lisa.

"When was the last time that I was here? Seems to me like ages!"

"You're right. It's been for a while."

"But everything looks the same."

"Just the things, Lisa. Nothing else is the same and never will be."

"So did you decide if we go out for a movie, or we'll watch something here? Elli?"

"I'm sorry, Lisa. What did you say?"

"Movie here, or we're going out?"

"Oh. I don't know. I wasn't really thinking about it."

"Okay then, we're going out. I don't feel like to, but you evidently needed to be taken out!"

"I guess there is no point to fight over it with you. But I'll make something good to eat for us first. I just don't feel like dining out."

"I'm in your hands. Make it a lot, and do it fast. I'm starving! At least at movie, I can be stuffed." Lisa knew, Elli cooks well.

"Do you wanna take a cab, or we'll take a walk back to your place?"

"We can walk. I'm glad the weather turned this way. We are not going to have many of this kind. So tell me about how everything is going with Nick."

"Oh, well. Here we go again. Elli, I feel ridiculous right now." "Why?"

"Do you know how many times did you ask me that question since we became friends? I feel ashamed."

"Not sure about how many times I asked about Nick."

"Elli, you know what I meant. Your questions about someone that I was with in a relationship. Well, at least I thought I am."

"For what? That you were giving a try to guys who were not worth it?"

"Well, yeah. Just thinking of how many I was giving a try, even when my instinct was telling me, 'No!' 'Forget it!' 'Run away!'"

"At least you did give it a try. Sometimes you just don't know till you do it. Look at me and ... Danny. I thought of him like my opposite. But he made me fall in love even with the sports. I enjoyed so much to spend the time outdoor with him— on the bike, walking, hiking— whatever. I learned from him to enjoy the sunlight, the rain, the snow ... and now he's gone." Elli's eyes filled up with tears too fast for her to hold it. At this time, she didn't even try it. "He loved the life so much, Lisa."

"Not as much as he loved you, Elli."

They both gave each other hug and started walking slowly toward Elli's place.

"But I wasn't going to talk to you about that. All I was trying to say is, when you don't give a try, later you might wonder how it could be... if you didn't let pass by the one who was worth it to stick with through good but what's most important through tough time as well. Looking back, every day with Danny was worth it. I'm—I was—the lucky one he didn't give up on me after many times of turning him down. That's why it hurts so badly that he's gone."

"I guess you are right. So, Nick, well, I do have to admit so far we had no drama going on in our, should I say, relationship. He is divorced, and as you know, he has a daughter. He's trying hard to still be involved in her life. I didn't meet her yet. And I'm okay with it. We are still not long enough together. So there is no reason to mess her head. She needs to know that even when Mom and Dad don't live with her together, they will be forever her mom and her dad. He has no problem to talk about it with me, so I have no feeling about him hiding something away from me. And he is making time for me. For us."

"It's been a while since you both got together. So is it love?"

"Love? Elli, honestly, what's the meaning of that word? I do think about him. I like to spend the time with him. Chemistry is great. I'm just not the same. I don't know if I'll be ever able to be spontaneously running toward someone, wrapping my arms without question on my mind, 'Isn't this too much,' after so many falls. But I have to admit—thanks to you and Danny I do believe— there is something special for all of us. It's just probably in different form for everybody. Maybe this is the most for me. But if yes, I'm fine with it."

"I know. It sort of sucks to get attached, to get used to someone, and then to deal with the reality that that someone is not there anymore. It's painful and takes so much energy to get up every day and keep going. I'm not even talking about the moving-on part."

"Danny will be so proud of you, Elli. That's what he loved about you. I'm sure it wasn't the only thing. But once, he mentioned how he likes about you, the inside strength. And your kindness to everyone. Even the losers."

"Lisa!"

"Sorry, but it's true. Some people just don't deserve to even have your attention. That's what I think. But you are too good, too kind to the people who you meet. But it's not worth it to make jerks to feel better. They are who they are. They choose it."

"Well, but sometimes even them may not be always who they are now. And maybe someone or something in their life turns them to be this way. And maybe something or someone will turn them to be better."

"I don't know. Now I only know I'm ready for a one superhot shower!"

"You've got it. Since you are a guest, you go first. Just don't be too long. I would love to take one as well before I'll fall asleep."

Elli brought fresh towel and washcloth to Lisa. "Shampoo and shower gel, you will see on the tub."

"Thanks."

While Lisa was taking a shower, Elli went to the kitchen to deal with what they left after dinner before they went to see the movie. Dishes were clean and put away in few minutes, and then she set up the tea cups and the wine glasses out on the countertop. Elli moved peacefully her body from the kitchen to the bedroom where she prepared the bed and set out her comfy nightclothes.

"I'm out! It's all yours!"

"Perfect timing."

"I didn't know what you will feel more like to. Cup of tea or glass of wine. So I put them both out," said Elli while heading out of the bathroom. She already wore her nightclothes.

"I don't know. Both sounds good," said Lisa while taking her favorite spot on the sofa.

"I like to have a tea."

"Then do one for me too. Thanks. And what are you wearing?"

"What? Oh. Yeah. It's Danny's. It was ... it was hard to fall asleep when he, but when I started to wear this shirt, it's so comfy, and I don't even know sometimes when or how I fell asleep. Here is our tea."

They woke up into a sunny Saturday morning. The air felt a little bit fresh and breezy, but the sun was promising a good weather day.

"Hope that breeze won't turn to the ugly wind bringing thousands of the clouds with it!" said Lisa while standing by the window.

"We will see. Now let's focus on the breakfast menu. Do you feel more like for the sweet or salty?"

"Coffee for sure. Anything else doesn't really matter. I can even have something from both."

"Ugh!"

"What?"

They both started to laugh. While eating, Elli started to lose the color from her face.

"Elli, what's wrong?"

"Nothing. What do you mean?"

"You just look like you had been eating white chalk for breakfast."

Before Lisa could finish the sentence, Elli excused herself and disappeared in the bathroom. By the time she did return to the kitchen, she found Lisa's seat empty.

"Lisa? Lisa, where are you? I'm back!" But she didn't hear any answer back, so she went through the whole apartment to look for her. She was nowhere to be found. Then she went to the hallway where she didn't see Lisa's shoes, so she went for her cellphone to call her. However, she could hear the ringing from Lisa's phone clearly coming from the bedroom. "I guess I just have to wait for her to come back." That didn't take long.

"Where have you been?"

"Just in the first store in the neighborhood."

"What for?"

"Here," said Lisa while she stretched out her hand with little box toward Elli. "I would like you to go and do it now. You know me how I am. Last few days, it's all narrowing to this little box. And I'm pretty sure it did cross your mind as well."

Elli just sat there with tears in her eyes. Lisa was still standing there with her hand stretched out.

"Come on, Elli. It's better to know. Then you can face it whatever the result will be."

"I can't."

"Of course you can! And you will. Look at me. You are not alone. I'm here for you no matter what."

In the moment of silence, Elli did reach out with her shaking hand for the box and disappear again in the bathroom.

"Elli?" Lisa knocked gently on the door. "Elli? Can I come in?" No answer. Silence. "I'm coming in," said Lisa, almost whispering. The doors were not locked. She found Elli sitting on the floor staring at the pregnancy test result. Her bottom lip was trembling. Her nose was all red as well as her eyes. The mascara was long time gone in the roll of toilet paper piling up in pieces beside her.

"So? Yes or no?"

Elli didn't say a word and just handed the test results to Lisa to see on her own.

"Oh my!" Lisa slid down on her knees and gave a tight hug to Elli.

"What's next? What am I supposed to do next? You asked me to take test. I did. What should I do next, Lisa?"

"How do you feel about it?"

"I ... I don't know. I'm not sure—yet. We both wanted it so much, and now it's real, but Danny isn't here. He will never know we ... I ..."

"Shhh. Slow down. Breathe. You don't have to make any decision right now. At this moment. You'll still need to go to see the doctor to be sure. Just remember that I'm here for you no matter what kind of decision you will make. Come. I'll make you a tea."

They didn't go anywhere but spent the whole morning chatting on the sofa. Elli's eyes did dry out after hours of crying. Her eyelids were so puffed up, so it was hurting her just to keep them open. By eleven o'clock, she fell asleep with her head resting on Lisa's shoulder. Lisa slipped out slowly while supporting Elli's head with the nearest pillow. She turned both of their cellphones silent. Then she realized she had made plans for tonight with Nick. She wrapped herself in the blanket and stepped out on the small balcony to make a quick phone call.

"Nick? Hi."

"Hi, Lisa. It's so good to hear your voice."

"Yours too, Nick. Listen. I know we have made plans for tonight, but—"

"Is something wrong?"

"If you will let me finish, you will know," said Lisa with a more relaxed voice than when she started the phone call. After that, Nick went quiet, and she retold to him shortly how everything went.

"I understand. And I'm sorry to hear that. I know I didn't meet Elli yet, but from your talk, I think she's pretty cool person."

"She is. And she's the strongest person I ever met. I don't understand why this ... why this must be happening to her! I'm so mad!"

"Maybe it's happening, so she'll be more happy at the end."

"She was happy with Danny. Now with him, they'll be happy, three of them if—"

"Lisa, just stay with her. Show her you are her true friend who'll support her. But let her make her own decision and accept it no matter what it'll be."

"I'm trying, Nick. I'm just not so strong as she is."

"This time, you have to. Don't think about yourself. This isn't about you. This is all about Elli and her decision which either way will change her life forever."

"Thanks, Nick. I'm glad to have you. Sorry for not be able to meet you tonight."

"Don't worry about that. We'll meet some other time. Just call me or txt me later. Whenever you'll have time. Would you?"

"I will. I gotta go."

"Okay."

"Bye, Nick."

"Talk to you soon, Lisa."

She sat down in one of the two small chairs in charming setup on the balcony with few pots and with little needle tree and few bright-colored plants. Elli's touch. She made everything so much to call for relaxation. The nearest tree offered beautiful view on its yellow-colored leaves. Lisa sigh quietly with the little breeze in the air and got up slowly and headed to the door back to where she left Elli. "Hey. You are up! Hungry?"

"Actually I am.

"Do you want me to fix something or make an order?"

"No. I'm fine. I'll do the early lunch dish for us."

"Sounds good to me already."

Chapter 3

"Hey."

"Hi."

"How's everything going?"

"I feel so lost. Trying to make the decision."

"Did you go see the doctor?"

"Yes. Now I have it on the paper. I still have time to make decision if I will—"

"Are you considering the interruption?"

"I'm trying not to. It just hurts so much to think of it if I won't do it. The kid will never see Danny. Will never have chance to talk to its daddy. Kids will be asked to make a picture of family, and there will be just the kid and me on it. Me and Mommy. No grandma, grandpa, aunts, uncles. But I feel like we belong together, and we both deserve the chance to be trying our best to live happy. Means a lot to me already. Do you think I'm crazy if I will decide to keep it?"

"No. Actually, I think you will be the best mommy for the little one. And you actually have already on the picture one more person, Aunt Lisa."

"Lisa, you are the best."

"Just for the credit, being a mommy, I heard, it's not always easy. I'm not trying to scare you away, but it's a lot of hard work. Exhausting. But on the other hand, when you'll hold it, when you'll look at the asleep face, when it'll call you a mommy, must be the best—"

"Lisa, am I missing something?" Elli started to giggle.

"I think I'm getting jealous. Well, if you keep it, I'll have the best right, the right to spoiled the kid. And then let you deal with parenting."

"That's the Lisa which I know!"

"Nick is picking me up today. Would you like to join us for a short walk and some food?"

"Not today. I feel a little bit tired already. But I would love to say hi to him finally. I'm sorry I wasn't able to meet him sooner."

"He'll be happy to meet with you!"

"Okay, just let me know when he'll be here, and I will walk with you out of building."

"Great!" Lisa was so happy they both will finally meet. She has been talking to each other about each other for a while.

"Nick! Nick! Hi! Let me introduce you to my very special friend Elli! Elli, Nick. Nick, Elli."

"Hello, Nick."

"Hello, Elli. It's finally so nice to meet you."

"You too. It feels like I already know you for a while."

"Oh no. Lisa did the report on me?"

"No, I did the research on who is stealing away my friend." All three of them started to laugh.

"Are you sure you are not coming with us?"

"Some other time, Lisa. I'm really falling apart right now. Need to go back to office, get finish one more order, and then I'm looking forward to a quick shower and a bed."

"Don't forget to eat something!"

"Yes, sir."

"Don't make joke about it. If I'll find out you skipped the meal, I'll be starting to make the check marks for it. And you know I will!"

"Yeah. I trust you."

"It was very nice to meet you, Elli."

"You too, Nick. Take good care of her."

"I will."

"Soooo? What do you think?"

"She is exactly how you described her. I believe she will be a great, happy mom."

"I hope so. She deserves the happiness, joy in her life."

Chapter 4

"Elli, Thanksgiving at my place."

"Don't you wanna be just with Nick and his kid?"

"He will see his kid after the holidays. He's ex-wife is taking her to Grandma and Grandpa."

"Then—"

"No. We can be alone together so many other days."

"Okay. Thank you. But I will bring some food with me. Please, let me know what will be my responsibility to show up with then."

"Deal."

"I'm so stuffed. All the way up to my ears! Coffee for anyone?" asked Nick.

"Didn't you say you are sooo stuffed?"

"I might find place for a little cup of coffee."

"Okay. I'll do it for you."

"No, no. You girls did all this. Let me do the coffee and a dessert."

"For me, just a half size and a—"

"Decaf. I know. I'm on it."

"Thank you, Nick."

"He is really good. I'm so happy you've got him a chance."

"Yeah, me too. He knows how to talk to me, how to make things better. I'm so sorry, Elli."

"What are you sorry for? Be proud of it, and don't let him go!"

"I won't."

"I would like to thank you very much for such a nice evening. I'm thankful to have both of you in my life. In our lives."

"The pleasure is on our side," said Nick while Lisa gave a squeezing hug to Elli.

"The cab is waiting. I'll walk you out to it."

"Thank you."

Chapter 5

"This is so exciting. That little bump is starting to show up! Are you planning to say anything about it soon at work?"

"Actually, tomorrow. I'll have my first picture to be taken."

"Can I come?"

"Would you like to?"

"I would love to!"

"I'll be happy to have you with me. Will you be okay to take some time off the work?"

"No problem! What time is your appointment?" "Twelve, our lunchtime," said Elli with a smile.

"I'm so happy you took me with you! The picture came out very nicely. Too bad we were not able to see the sex of the baby. It was like it's playing with us. Hide- and-seek."

"I'm not sure if I really want to find out what it's going to be. At the end, it doesn't really matter. All what matters is that it's healthy. Growing good."

"I know. That is the most important. But if we know, we can look for clothes. You can choose the name and talk to the baby by it."

"Silly. Clothes we can look up for neutral colors— which might be good for both of them. And names, we can talk about for boy and for a girl. I heard that did happen before, that somebody was ready for a girl or a boy, and the opposite happened!"

"I know. Life is sometimes playing funny games with people!"

"Yeah! There is no guarantee in life. That's for sure."

"You are so strong, Elli. I'm so proud of you."

"Nick was wondering if you have any idea for Christmas holidays. I know we just have Thanksgiving, but it'll go fast. You know!"

"I didn't think about that yet. My life is about visiting Danny's grave, baby's doctor's appointments, work, and you guys."

"We thought so. So Nick came up with idea to rent out a place. Just close by in Wisconsin. With fireplace. He can take day trip to ski so we can chat and relax. Low- key. He'll see his daughter before holidays. By the way, he would like me to meet her. I'm not sure if this is his best idea. Especially in holiday time like this."

"Don't you wanna go, just two of you? You don't need me to kill the romance in front of the fireplace."

"Are you kidding? No. Absolutely no. We would miss you there. These are the family holidays. And as you know, there's not much as family for neither of us around. We three—sorry, soon four—we are family. I know. It's not like through blood, but you know what I mean! So what do you think? To me it sounds great! We will escape that gift-haunting craziness of most of the people. All we need is pack some good food and warm clothes."

"I'll think about it."

"Okay. You think, and I'll tell Nick to start working on it so we have few places to choose from."

That day, Elli stopped by at Danny's grave. There was a little chill in the air, but Elli didn't mind. She closed her coat all the way up and pulled down her hat over her ears to keep warm as long as possible. She looked at his picture. She missed him so much. The wave of pain shook her body while her eyes filled up with tears. She was thinking about the whole day—picture of their kid which he will not able to be around, the first holidays without him, the idea of getaway for Christmas with Lisa and Nick, the words from Lisa about being so strong.

"Danny, I can't anymore. I'm not so strong as Lisa sees me! If it won't be her and Nick, I'll be probably never getting so far on my own. I still feel you in our place. I'm still hoping for you to pop out from somewhere there on me. I'm not losing my sanity, not at least what I know. But I just wish so badly to be able to hold you, to be able to talk to you, or to just sit with my legs across yours on our sofa with book in my hands and newspaper in yours." When Elli realized her whole body was shaking terribly from cold and stress, she looked at Danny's picture one more time and moved her body slowly toward her car. Before she started walking away from Danny's grave, she made a promise in silence—that she'll do her best for their child.

Before Nick and Lisa were going to pick her up with all her stuff already packed, she had special Christmas cookies and all kinds of traditional food in boxes in the fridge from yesterday. Today, she will be having no time to put it all together. She left the work sooner to get to her doctor's appointment before the trip. Elli just wanted to make sure all goes well and if there is something that she should avoid at all. But she was shocked by another unexpected news. She wasn't expecting one boy or girl. The doctor said she can clearly hear two heartbeats. Elli had to take a sip of water from the nurse to stop the dizziness. She couldn't believe it. How ironic. If Danny was there by her side, all of it would be such a blessing. No worries but joy. Now her brain felt like it's going for a race.

The nurse checked out her pressure while asking a question, if she'll be all right to drive. They all knew her story from Lisa. That's why they were all around her for the news.

Elli was only able to repeat one question. "How come we didn't see it, didn't hear it, didn't know it at the beginning?"

The doctor didn't answer right away Elli's question. Instead, she asked, "If you know, would you do anything different?"

Elli knew there was only one answer she could honestly have on her mind. The answer would be no! She knew, even if she'll hear there are three more, she won't change a thing.

She said, "Thank you for the water. I'm good now."

"Are you sure?"

"If I'm sure? I just made a promise at Danny's grave— felt like yesterday—that I'll do my best for our child. And now you're asking me if I'm sure that I'm okay? Do I have any other way than be okay—than be sure I'm okay? I was sure I can be a good mommy for one. How on earth I'm supposed to know if—" At this moment, Elli broke into heavy crying. She sat back down.

"Elli, can your friend come pick you up? I have strong faith that at the end, it will be all right. You have very strong personality. You are focused, you are organized, and you are realistic. If anybody can do it, it's you! I know it's just been for you, bump after bump on the road. But you will handle it. Can we call some of your friends?" Dr. Raysse suggested.

Elli just pulled out her phone from her purse like a robot and dialed Lisa's number. But she didn't feel like she'll be able to talk, so she handed it to the doctor.

Lisa was there shortly with Nick. They already heard the twin news over the phone conversation with the doctor. Since Lisa was having the key from Elli's place now, they did fast stop for all the things for their getaway. They knew if they will be going from the doctor there, she will be having no strength to go.

"Hi, Elli. We are here. Come."

"Do you need anything to be signed or to be paid?" Nick asked the doctor, while Lisa helped Elli with her coat.

"No. We have all what we need. Thank you for coming. If you'll need anything, here is my cell number. You can call me anytime. She refused to take any medication for calming her down."

"Thank you, doctor. We will take care of her."

During the drive to Wisconsin, they all kept in silence. Just holiday songs were quietly played as a background. After arriving, they forced Elli to get to bed to get some sleep. Then they unpacked all the stuff from the car. Nick started the fire in the wood-burning fireplace, while Lisa put away the food.

"Are you hungry or thirsty, Nick?"

"Truly, not much, but we should have a little bit of both. We need to be strong for her."

"Nick, what we will do? I have no idea what I'll be doing without you. I'll be now probably sitting with Elli in her apartment and crying through the whole holidays."

"All is going to be all right," Nick said and hugged Lisa that was already shaking. "Lisa," Nick started, almost whispering. "I have to—I, I mean I would like to get you something now. I was waiting for the perfect moment, but I realized that any moment with you is perfect. Even when we have to deal with my ex, with my struggles not to be able to be more with my kid, Elli, job, whatever. I know there's no one else with who I would like to get through all this. I know we both were hurt many ways, but we managed together to laugh again. To be truthful with each other. I feel this is real." By these words, Nick held out a ring in front of Lisa. She was shocked—happy but shocked.

"You don't have to say anything. Just please, can I put the ring on your finger? I would love to marry you, Lisa. I don't know when. You know I still don't have finalized divorce papers about few more things. But I want you to know my true feelings."

Lisa did let Nick put the ring on her finger. She was crying and smiling at the same time.

"Nick, I love you. I couldn't wish for any more amazing men to be in my life than you. Promise you'll never stop working on our relationship."

"You have my word, Lisa. I promise."

Still in the hug, they both sit without moving and were staring in the crackling wood in the fireplace.

"We should go get some sleep. Elli is going to need us tomorrow."

"I know."

In the morning, Elli woke up quietly and started preparing pancakes for breakfast. "Good morning," Elli said to them when they appeared by her. "I just didn't know if you would like to have them with veggies or with sweet jam and whipped cream." "Thank you so much. You are amazing!"

"You did all the unpacking. Sorry that I wasn't able to help."

"Come on, Elli! You are taking care of us enough! Thank you so much. How are you?"

"I'm better now. Thank you both that you didn't let me stay at home."

"Hey, girls, how does walk after breakfast sounds?" asked Nick.

"I think that's the greatest idea!"

Elli spotted the ring on Lisa's finger. "Congratulations! I hope I'm right about the ring. Is it that what I think?" said Elli while looking from one to another one with a smile on her face.

"Yes, it is. We don't know when. First, of course, he needs to finish his divorce."

"I know. It'll be all right. You two are great together."

"Thank you so much, Elli. That means a lot to me from you."

While packing for leaving back to Illinois, Nick asked Lisa and Elli if they would like to stop for a meal break on the way. Since both of them were not able to give him an answer, he decided for all of them.

"We will make a stop to eat."

None of them said a word. All of them were lost in their own thoughts. After they placed orders for meal, Nick surprised both of them.

"I was thinking ... I was thinking how things are, how they might go. How everything will change. What do you think, Lisa, Elli, if we will look up for two townhouses together or at least close to each other? I would love Lisa to live with me, and you and your two little ones will be easier to help out if we'll be closer than now. We all will still keep the privacy."

"I think that's the excellent idea. What do you think, Elli?"

"I don't know it now. I just feel like I need to stay in Danny's and my place."

"But remember, even you and Danny, you were talking and searching for a place to move."

"I know."

"Okay. You know what. Idea is out. Let it sit on our minds, and we will talk about it later by the end of the week. Can it be?"

"Okay."

"Okay."

Elli was so happy to be home. She fixed herself cup of tea. Nick was continuing driving Lisa home. So they didn't stay. But they both felt like Elli will be all right now.

Lisa smiled about the thought that probably at the same time, they are all doing the same thing—unpacking. She grabbed the phone.

"Elli? Hi. How are you?"

"You won't believe. I'm all unpacked. Sipping tea. Laundry is in process. How about you?"

"I started laundry too, but I'll take care of clean clothes later. Just emptied the bag, and now I'm sitting down. Too tired to move. Sorry. I shouldn't be the one complaining!"

"Why not? Just because you're not expecting twins, you can't be tired?"

"I had a good time with both of you."

"Nick did surprise you. Am I right?"

"Completely."

"I'm very happy for you. One less thing to worry about!"

"You're so silly. I'm so blessed to have you both. I'll see you tomorrow at work."

"Yes. See you there!"

Chapter 6

Snow covered everything early morning with light layer. In combination with sunshine, Elli, on her way to the work, turned the steering wheel sharply in the direction to the beach. Her car was the only one taking the spot alongside the sugary-looking beach. View was breathtaking. Every step on slightly frozen sand leaning closer to the lake made her relaxed.

"I miss you so much, Danny. Forgive my weakness. I'm trying to be strong for both of them. I know I have wonderful people around me. I shouldn't be complaining at all. I just don't know if … I need you back by my side. That's all what I wish for, I need you so much. Last year, we were here together stepping over frozen waves … Your arms tied around me, and I felt with you, nothing could go wrong—all unbreakable. Why today I can hardly breathe? How can I put myself together when I feel so broken into pieces inside? Instead of one, there will be two kids. Two little special human beings. I love them so much already. Will be that enough?" Elli felt a chill shivering her whole body, so she started to walk back to the car, wiping tears with the end of the sweatshirt sleeve sticking out from her coat.

"Hey, where have you been for so long, Elli?" said Lisa that was already checking over the last-hour empty chair at Elli's desk.

"Hi. I was … I did stop by the lake for a walk."

"Are you crazy? Didn't you check today's temperature?"

"No."

"Well, you should start to do these things. If not for you, then for them!"

"I'm sorry, okay? I'm sorry for not checking the temperature, I'm sorry for not being perfect, I'm sorry for not being strong enough, and I'm sorry just for being sorry. I'm so tired, Lisa. I'm tired of this life. I'm very tired of myself!"

"Come here. It's been lately too much to handle by yourself. Did you have a chance to think about what Nick said?"

"Said about what?"

"Said about looking for living spaces for us close to each other."

"No. I didn't. Wasn't time. I need to stay at Danny's and my place."

"Elli, he'll be with all of you everywhere. I'm sure he'll be happy if you'll have us closer."

"I'm not ready to move, Lisa. I'm so sorry."

"That's okay. Don't be sorry. I'm just worried I won't be there when you're gonna need me. That's all."

"Nick, hi. Here is Lisa. I think you can start searching for those two close living spaces, as you mentioned. I think she needs to let go of their place. She's going so low. She's not trying to reach out for any help. I'm so worried about her now. I still believe in her strong personality. But you must agree she had to deal with too much lately. How much she had been through! What else she'll be able to face it? And seeing her today, we must move things forward!"

"I know. But, Lisa, don't push her! She needs to be ready to let go to move. I think she knows that. I think she does understand that letting go, it'll be the only way to survive and get stronger. If not for herself, then for the babies."

"When is her next doctor appointment?"

"By the end of January."

"Make sure you'll go with her."

"Of course I will."

"Not if you won't know the date."

"I'll find out."

"Lisa, I had to go now. I'm sorry."

"It's okay."

"When I'll have a moment, I'll start to look for those places. I'm happy you're not afraid to move in with me. I love you. Will I see you tomorrow?"

"Yes. I gotta go too. So see you tomorrow."

Chapter 7

"Elli, all looks good. Your pregnancy goes well. Their heartbeats are like strong drums. Are you eating enough? Your weight should be slightly higher. Any problem with eating?"

"None. I'm just trying to eat more vegetables and fruits."

"Okay. That's fine. Just don't skip any meal. Keep taking your prenatal vitamins, and here is another picture. Would you like to know the sex of the babies?"

"Yes!"

"No!"

"Sorry, Lisa, if the mother still doesn't want to know—"

"I know! I was just hoping she did change her mind about it. Evidently, not yet. I will try next time."

"Why don't you just give up on that?"

"Why? I'm too excited about it. I wanna know. I can't wait until May. That's like forever."

"Nothing will change if we'll know."

"Oh yeah. It will."

"I need to get your focus on something else! Thank you, doctor. So I'll see you in a month."

"If everything will go like until now, then yes. If anything, any even slight change, please call the office or stop by."

"Okay. I will. Thanks."

"We will. Thank you, doctor. Bye."

"Bye."

"She's nice."

"Yes. I trust her. She seems to be always on the top of everything and accurate."

"And organized." They both started to smile about that. Dr. Raysse was too organized. Everything had always the same spot every time they went to her office.

"Oh well. We all have something. Plus it's better she's this way. Can you imagine the opposite?"

"You won't be going there with those precious cuties. Look at them. They look so comfy by each other," said Lisa, looking at the ultrasound picture of the twins. "You are so amazing, Elli. Thank you so much for letting me to be a part of it. I love them already so much!"

"Me too, Lisa. They are just too many changes to adjust. To accept."

"But it's all worth it. Remember that! Don't fall apart for little everyday things. When you'll feel you can't take it anymore, look at it as a whole picture. How it will be when longer time will pass by."

"Hope I'll remember that when I'll be lost between laundry, feedings, showers."

"If you'll not, I'll be there to remind you that."

"Lisa, will you go with me to pick the cribs over the weekend?"

"This weekend, Nick has his daughter. We are taking her to the waterpark. Just for a little escape from the cold winter weather. I was just about to ask you if you feel like to come with us."

Katie, Nick's daughter, was a pleasant little girl to have around. From beginning, she was very quiet. As the time passed, she started to accept the reality staying with mom and seeing her dad whenever possible. She started to have a good connection with Lisa and did enjoy to have Elli around as well. They all became a very important people of her little girl's world with parents not living anymore in one household. With Lisa's happy, optimistic personality and Elli's kind approach to people, it was only a matter of time when Katie will feel ease of her sorrow.

"Katie is very excited. And since there is still good amount of snow, we will take her sledding or skiing. Depends what she'll feel for. If you'll come, I'll go with you to the pool or to the lazy river, and Nick can spend one-on-one time with her on snow."

"It's gonna be a blast for sure. I just feel this week somehow drained that's why I figure the low-key project got over it."

"Low-key project? Are you kidding me? The cribs for them are very important! They will spend lots of time in them for a long term."

"I know, I know. I did good research, but I would like to see them in reality."

"Sorry, you did sound like let's walk to the first store and get over with it. That just wasn't you at all. We can go for crib hunting next weekend. Let's do the getaway this one. Please."

"What about this? You'll enjoy with Katie and Nick getaway weekend. I'll make nothing except relax in those two days. And I promise I will not go to the store to look for cribs. We will do it next weekend together. How's that sound?"

"Are you sure? I don't want you to feel lonely, and we will be out of here. But still. It's only few hours of driving. So if anything—and I mean anything—call us. Okay?"

"Lonely? Are you kidding me? That will be my special word … which I'll probably not use in a long time. Oh well. Yes. I will call you. But I think I'm looking forward to a one peaceful weekend. And I think the weather forecast is not so well, so it'll be probably good to just stay in anyway."

"Okay. If you are sure, I won't force you. We will keep in touch, and we will stop by when we will be back."

Chapter 8

"Finally, Saturday morning!" thought Elli while setting stuff for breakfast. There were no signs of sun coming out, but she was still in a good mood. She turned on the music while she sat down with a steaming cup of tea.

"Looks like pretty soon, I'll be in need to push the table forward so I can fit in without bumping myself every time I'll go sit down ... and on my way out too." She made a smile by thinking about herself how she'll look in a month or two. Finally, she could enjoy full table of food for breakfast without any rush away from it.

"Can't believe I eat so much. Now I don't need more place for getting up but crane for lifting." Her only plan for weekend was hunting for cribs. Now she had no clue how to fill up those two days. Her place was small and organized. Little bit dusty, but she was not in the mood for cleaning. She turned on the TV, but nothing really caught her attention. "Gosh, I should really go with them to Wisconsin."

"Hi, Lisa. How's everything going?"

"Hi. Katie is evidently having a good time. Somehow I got tired, so I let them enjoy daddy-daughter time on the hill. There is still so much snow! I should join them later for lunch, and in the afternoon, we'll go to waterpark. How about you?"

"Hmm. I don't know yet. Weather is just so-so. TV, nothing. I have no idea yet. But for sure, I don't feel like to do any cleaning."

"Do you want me to come for you?"

"Are you out of your mind? I'll find something to do. You just enjoy yourself over there, and you may send me some pictures of you guys. Say hi to Katie and Nick from me, okay?"

"I will. And if anything, call me, all right?"

"Yes, sir. I'll call you if something."

After they finished their conversation, Elli dropped the phone on the sofa beside her and rested her back against the cushions. She sat like that for a few minutes. No better idea than go to do the grocery shopping. "Let's get over with!"

On the way to the store, she answered a phone call from work. So instead of short drive to do grocery, she took direction automatically toward her work.

"Elli! Elli, hi! Over here! Thank you very much for coming. We were not able to get some orders out of computer. I'm sure you'll remember them and will help us out while a technician will fix them."

"No problem. Which one they are? Do you have order number or company who ordered?"

"Sure! Here it is."

"Oh. Yeah. This one was done last week. I do remember."

"That's wonderful. They did call us with some questions, which we were not able to answer without computer … or you."

"Let me get my coat off."

"Elli, you didn't leave? Was there any big issue to deal with?"

"No. No! Not at all. All is in order now. I just thought while I'm here, I'll use the time to do something extra."

"You should go home. Recharge energy. How is everything going? Must be hard. Sorry. Don't want you to feel bad. We all think how amazing person you are to not give up."

"Didn't feel so amazing when my belly was pushing the table with breakfast," said Elli with a smile. "How am I? Hmm. Hard to say. Looks like I have to deal with one surprise after another one. But I'm sure this is still nothing compared to how it's gonna be when these will be born. It's going so fast, and I'm not ready. But I don't know if there is anything to help me to get ready."

"I understand. But once more, you are amazing to all of us. And if there is anything with which we might be able to help you, please, let us know."

"Thank you."

"We are happy to have you here."

By the time Elli was leaving the office building, it got completely dark and colder outside, so she tied up her coat closer to her body to keep the heat. Even with belly growing each day, she still had the look that turned the heads to her direction. While walking, she heard the phone ringing in her bag. It was Nick.

"Hi, girl! How is our favorite auntie doing? I'll put you on speaker so you don't have to repeat over and over to everyone here."

"Hi, Elli!"

"Hey there!"

She heard happy voices of Katie and Lisa.

"Hi, everyone. It's so good to hear your voices! Me. I'm okay. You tell me. Katie, are they being fun to be with or they running out of energy?"

"Elli, good guessing. They are trying to take shifts," Katie said and giggled. "It is fun! We did have a good time so far."

"Glad to hear that. Be patient with them. You know we older people … I'm sure they're trying their best."

"I will."

"Hey, what older people?" Lisa stepped into their conversation. How are you, girl? What are you up to now?"

"I'm just walking to the car." In that moment, Elli slipped.

"Aah!"

"What happened?"

"I'm okay. I just slipped on those stairs in the garage by work—you know which one. But I caught the balance."

"What? What on earth are you doing there? I knew I shouldn't leave you there or at least stay at home with you."

"What for? Then you'll be missing all the fun there, and you'll be forced to come along to work with me. They had some problem with PC and were lost in some paperwork. So I stopped by."

"And stayed till now!"

"It's okay. I'll put my feet up tomorrow. Promise."

"Good girl. You know we're coming tomorrow. So …"

"Cookies and milk will be ready."

"Silly. How's the weather there? We catch the beautiful one. I'll txt you the picture which Nick took when they were leaving the hill with Katie. Amazing sunset."

"Can't wait!"

"Did you make it safe to the car?"

"Yes. I'm in."

"Okay. Drive safe. If we won't call you, we for sure will see you when we'll get back tomorrow."

"Can't wait to see you. Have more fun and drive back safe."

"We sure will!"

On Sunday, Elli felt so tired after breakfast that she, for first time, didn't eat in the kitchen. She took all what she wanted to the living room. She covered herself with soft, warm blanket and started eating while trying to find something to watch on television. After a while, she was able to choose a movie. But since it was almost over, she ended up watching a home project. It crossed her mind how nice it'll be to have Danny by her side. Sometimes, they did that when they felt too lazy to be active. It was nice to see how dramatically can everything be changed by choosing the right colors and materials. Elli looked around herself and moved her hand slowly all over her showing belly.

"You two are being too quiet today. Rough night? Hard to believe I survived all your movements in the night! That's why I have no energy to move at all today. Who knows if I'll be even able to function tomorrow. I'll better not think about tomorrow. One day at a time!"

After few hours of being wrapped up, she couldn't hold it anymore, so she was forced to leave the comfort of her sofa. She decided to go for a walk at least till the washer cycle will ended so she'll get some move and fresh air.

The air was so cold she wished she didn't leave without the gloves. But she knew if she'll go back for them, she'll stay at home. She just pulled the sleeves out of her jacket as much as possible to cover her fingers with it. After few minutes, she felt good she went for a walk. Cold but refreshing. How lucky her apartment was cozy and warm, and she smiled thinking about it.

"I was so unrealistic to even think I could leave that place. It has all what I need. What we all will need. It's small, but it'll work out for now. I'll just finish the cleaning, reorganizing, and I'll be ready for you. Your daddy will be with us."

Elli got back home just in time to get clothes to the dryer and realized how fast it turned dark outside. With tea in her hands, she let her body slide down on the sofa and put her feet up. Before reaching for the blanket to cover herself, she freed her hands from the cup.

"Nick, she's not picking the phone."

"Maybe she's in the laundry room, or the TV is too loud."

"Oh, stop it! You know she'll have now phone with her when going to do laundry. And that with TV! Good one!"

"Try to call her later."

"I'm trying to do that for half an hour already. Should I call 911?"

"Calm down, Lisa. I'm sure Elli is okay. We should be there in about twenty-five minutes."

"You know what all can happen in twenty-five minutes?"

"Look at me. She is okay. Don't even let any bad thoughts cross your mind! We're going straight there. Katie would like to see her too, so we'll drop her at her mom's place after."

"Okay. I hope you're right."

"How many times did you ring the doorbell already? Feels too long for her to answer the door. She's still not picking up the phone. Just realized, I do have the key in my bag. I'll be right back."

"I'll keep ringing the doorbell."

Lisa rushed down the stairs to the car. Hope she is okay. She must be okay. Where is that key? Finally! Of course it has to be at the bottom of the bag. I can't believe it!"

"Nick, I got it! Nothing? No response?" asked Lisa while getting the key with shaking hand in the lock. Moments later, the door swung open, and Lisa stepped in with Nick and Katie right behind her.

"Elli! Elli! Where are you? Are you okay? Come on, girl!"

Lisa shook Elli's shoulder gently as possible but with urgency.

"Elli, are you okay? Say something! Please!"

"Lisa, what's going on? Ouch, my back!"

"Thank God! You won't believe how much you scared me, girl. Don't do that again! Don't do that ever again. I was trying to call you! Nick rang the bell like crazy! Are you okay?"

"I … I'm okay. Hi, guys!" said Elli toward Nick and Katie. "I was just out for a walk while doing the laundry. Laundry!"

"Forget about the laundry!"

"No, I still have the laundry in the dryer. I must have fallen asleep. It's so dark. What time is it? Oh no. I did fell asleep!"

"See, Lisa? Daddy was right!" said Katie while getting hug to Elli.

"Hi, Elli. Glad you're all right. You still have laundry downstairs?"

"Hi, Nick. Yes. I'll get it later. If it didn't bother anybody by now, it will be okay to leave it as it is till tomorrow. It got really late."

"What about this? Meanwhile, you'll straight your back and get us those promised cookies. I'll get you the laundry upstairs."

"You don't have to, Nick."

"That's okay."

"Nick will get you the laundry, and I'll get us all nice, warm tea, milk and cookies for Katie. You just tell us what you were up to today that knocked you out so much," Lisa said while finally smiled with relief at Elli.

"For me, milk, please," asked Katie.

After a while, they all sat around the table in the living room and enjoyed the snack and talk until it was time to get Katie home to her mom.

"All right, time to go," said Nick.

It was a very pleasant atmosphere, but it was getting late. Katie gave a last big hug to Elli before Lisa got up and started her speech.

"You know, you can call me anytime or Nick if you need anything. We will be right here! Don't leave the key in the door. Just in case."

"I know. I know. Thank you, Lisa. Thank you all. I'm very fortunate to have you. Drive safe, and I'll talk to you tomorrow. Katie, I'm very happy you had with them a good time. Next time I'll try to go, okay?" said Elli to Katie while getting her hug and one more cookie for the road.

"That's the deal. We did miss you! It's so funny to feel the babies move in your belly. We still didn't pick the names. You didn't pick them over this weekend, right?"

"No. I was waiting with it. I'm sure we'll pick the best together."

"But, Lisa, for sure cribs are next step. That'll be easier than names. I guess. Bye, guys!"

"Lisa, you should relax yourself a little bit," said Nick to Lisa after dropping off Katie at her mom's place. "I don't want Elli to deliver babies too early because of us."

"I almost got heart attack today! First, she didn't pick the calls, and then she didn't open the doors. I was going nuts, wasn't I?"

"Yes, you did, my lunatic." Nick ended the conversation with a laugh.

He was happy to be with Lisa alone after such a busy weekend. "Are you too tired?"

"It depends what's on your mind, Nick."

"Just trying to figure out—if I should just drop you off at home or if I should stay."

"No doubt about it. Of course stay! Finally, we have time for each other, and you're thinking about just dropping me home."

"Well, I didn't know how much you did wear out."

"Pretty much. Tell you the truth, but I'll be more relax by you." They looked at each other. While driving, Nick gave Lisa a firm hand squeeze. She felt happy instantly and enjoyed it till they got to her place.

"You were right, Nick. I don't want to scare Elli. It's just driving me crazy to know what she has been through and that she's getting closer to her due date."

"You're mine, silly. Her due date is in May."

"Don't forget what the doctor said. There's a big possibility her due date will be sooner, since she's expecting twins, plus all that stress on the top of it."

"Yes, you're right. But I guess thanks to you we're ready, even if she'll deliver today."

"Yeah, just make fun of me. You both. You'll thank me both for that how I am."

"Oh, I'm thanking every day since I met you for it, Lisa. I won't change a thing about you … maybe the middle night snoring," Nick said and started to laugh.

"I'm not snoring!"

"How do you know when you're asleep?"

"Oh, stop it!"

"I'm just teasing you." Nick finished their conversation with a passionate kiss.

Chapter 9

"Glad I can say, 'You can cross off another month.' All looks good to me."

"Thank you, doctor. It's hard to believe that. Feels like few weeks passed, not the months. First, it looked like it goes too slowly. Now I just want to stop or at least slow down the time."

"Remember what we talked last visit about? One day at a time. Those days when you were confused are gone. Looks like you pass that storm. I'm happy for you. Your kids will be one day very proud of you."

"Still not sure sometimes. I'm afraid of all possible things, and I'll break crying in the middle of the night. But then Lisa and Nick will appear, and I know there's no turning back. And I just must get through one more day and after that, another one. There will be always piece of Danny in them to get us all through. That's my hope for the present. Keep heading to the future. He's gone, but I still remember which things we wanted in the past. Thank you very much for reassuring me they're all right. Both. I can't wait to meet them. The pictures of them are so realistic but not a reality yet."

"Take good care of yourself and remember, one day at a time," said the doctor to Elli while getting her out of the ambulance to Lisa.

"Does she finally let you tell her the sex of the babies?" asked Lisa, wishing much for a positive answer from the doctor.

"What is your guess?"

"She didn't."

"Maybe next time, Lisa. We still have what, about three months to go." The doctor closed the door with a friendly smile.

"So you didn't ask again. Okay. So this weekend, we are gonna all write down two girls and two boys' names. Just because you and your stubbornness. What about work? What did the doctor say?"

"I don't know."

"Did you even ask?"

"I think I didn't."

"Then let's go back to her office."

"No. Lisa, wait. Kids are okay. I'm okay. She wants me to come back in a month. If something will not go right, I'll ask about it."

"Am I having your word on it?"

"Yes," Elli answered after a short pause.

"That didn't sound very reassuring but okay. For now."

"Thanks, Lisa. I got tired and hungry. What about you. Hungry?"

"Always."

So let's get something good. Neither of us needs to head back to the office. I'll just let Nick know how things went at the doctor."

"All right."

"Lisa. To these names. What about we all just write them down and will pick two of them when they'll be born?"

"That's probably the craziest idea I heard from you, but why not?"

"The food is so good! Great idea we took it with us. It'll be tough to walk right now home." Lisa smiled happily at Elli.

"I have good news too, Elli."

"You are pregnant!"

"No, not yet." Lisa hurried covered her disappointment about it with the news about Nick's divorce. "Nick's divorce. It's almost over. She realized it's the best for all of them this way.

They both will try keep Katie's life going as smooth as possible."

"That's great. Wish sometimes for some guidance for life. Wouldn't that be nice?"

"Yeah. I guess. Oh, Elli, remember how we talked about the townhouses close to each other? Nick found duplex."

"Lisa, I did think about it a lot. It sure sounds great, and no words can describe how I feel thankful for all of it—what you both did and still doing for me, for us."

"But ..."

"But in that little apartment, I still feel him. Trying to be strong. Danny is still here on my mind. It has been too long not to see his face, not to hold him, tease him, make him curious, crazy. When the strength is washing away, in here, I feel I'm not alone."

"I understand, but for sure, you'll not make anything easy for us to help you with."

"That was fun, guys! Thank you," said Elli.

"We should save this name writing for baby shower. Pardon. Correction. Babies shower."

Katie and Nick were just laughing happily. Looking at Elli, Lisa put all the little cards with names to one envelope.

"We have names, cribs, some clothes. We're good to go." Lisa smiled.

"No way. I'm not ready. I do, and I'm not. That's confusing, right?"

"Yeah. It sure is."

"Lisa, what Elli said about that duplex townhouse?"

"Of course no. She's not ready. She probably never will be. I have no idea what to do to change her mind. Wish I can just stop by, tell her let's pack everything, and move her before babies will be born. Can you imagine to move her when they'll be born? But she refused so strongly. She's so clear about staying."

"Well, then I don't see a way to change her mind right now. Not at this moment."

"That's so frustrating."

"I'm sure it's harder for her than for us. Don't forget about it. People will be watching. She'll be seeing him probably in the kids."

"Gosh. I just got a bad chill right now all over."

At 11:30 p.m., Lisa's phone rung on Nick's nightstand.

"What is … is that the phone? Now?"

"That's mine," said Lisa with a sleeping voice till the realization who was calling didn't hit her. Got her awake in second.

"Nick, hurry the phone! That's Elli!" Nick handed the phone to Lisa.

"Elli! Elli! Can you hear me?" Lisa asked with a shaking voice but no answer, except the phone rang again.

"Press the answer button, sweetheart."

"Very funny!" said Lisa moodily while pressing answering button.

"Elli, are you okay?"

The long and quiet pause in the phone was interrupted by Elli's heavy crying and didn't get Lisa to answer till Elli did blow her nose.

"Lisa, please come. Please come, Lisa, please."

"Are you okay, Elli? Are the babies okay?" Lisa tried to find out what's going on over the phone, but no answer was coming back. She could hear just heartbreaking cry. "I'll be there, Elli. Hold on. Whatever it is, it's gonna be all right. Everything's gonna be okay. Stay with me on line, please!"

"Nick, I gotta go. This is not good."

"What did Elli say?"

"She only said, 'Lisa, please come. Please come, Lisa. Please.'" "I'll take you there."

"No, I'm okay. I mean ... I think I should get to her by myself. Alone. I'm sorry. I can't explain it, Nick. It's just the feeling."

"I understand. Please, drive safe and call me anytime. I might fall asleep, but don't give up on me and keep calling till you'll get me on line."

"Okay. I will. I love you."

Lisa sped up on the empty roads, not really sure if she did or did not even pass the crossroad on red. She could barely breathe. She kept holding the phone tight with her terribly shaking hand, which was the only connection between her and Elli. None of them was able to talk. Elli just kept crying heavily. Lisa could feel very deep sorrow out of the cry. Her foot automatically pushed more and more on the speed till she reminded herself of the urge to get safely to Elli.

She left the car parked across two parking lots and ran to Elli's apartment. She didn't even knock on the door. In the phone, she could hear her still crying, so she pulled out the key and opened the door by herself.

"Elli, I'm here."

She saw Elli sitting on the closet floor with some shoe box open and holding many Post-it paper cards with notes—notes from Danny. It was definitely Danny's handwriting on all of them. Through all of it, she saw what Elli went through; she never saw her looking so lost, so fragile. She could almost feel the pain in the air. She crushed down on her knees and hugged Elli tight.

"I'm here, Elli. I'm here now. I'm here for you." Lisa kept repeating over and over again while hugging Elli tight. After a while, one Post-it sticker got her full attention. It was a beautiful text with Danny's handwriting and another one and another ... whole big pile surrounding Elli, with his thoughts written over his last days to Elli about her pregnancy.

None of them could stop crying. None of them could stop reading notes over and over again.

The more they read, the more they cried.

Both of them stopped crying deeply past midnight. No strength left. No tears could get out of their heavily swollen eyes. They were not able to talk. The first words spoken with heavily hoarse voice came out of Elli. "He knew. Danny knew. He knew before I even started thinking about it as a possibility. I missed him so much. I can't live without him. It hurts so badly. Whole body ..." Elli sobbed. "I feel it's gonna explode. I can't, Lisa. I'm none without him."

Lisa kept holding her through the entire time. She was still speechless. Danny's simple notes were too breathtaking. Elli's body kept trembling strongly.

"I can't ... I don't want to live without Danny anymore. All that being strong was just a pose. Not real. I'm too broken without him. So real. All. Now only just a dream. I wish he can come back. I will give everything what I can, but it just won't change a thing.

All is dark. There's no light to break it through that darkness anymore. Every move hurts so badly. I have no strength, no desire to keep going like that."

"Elli, everything's gonna be easier. Everything's gonna be all right. I'm here. Nick too. Katie loves you and needs you too. And of course, the babies too! This knocked me down too. I still have chills from Danny's notes. They're so beautiful. I probably never did, and I'll probably never will read something so heartbreaking in my life. But look how Danny was happy just by a thought of a possibility that you really are pregnant. He ... for him, you'll the best mom of all. He even made a tip ..." Lisa's voice broke in the middle of the sentence. "He even thought you'll have twins and make names, plans."

"But now it's just all gone. Forever. I'm too tired. I feel empty, useless. It's so hard to breathe. Hope is gone followed by faith. Nothing is left. Emptiness."

"Shhh. Elli. Shhh. Tomorrow will be better. And then every day will be better, little by little. I promise. You're hurt too badly right now, but look how far you've got. Everything happens for a reason. There is so much love coming out of his notes. Take the happiness and strength out of them. Don't burry yourself into sadness. That's just not you!"

Lisa carefully scooped up all of Danny's notes and placed them into the box which Elli was still having on her lap.

"Come on Elli, get up, please. You need to help me with that. You three are getting a little bit too heavy for me to lift up."

"I'm sorry."

"Don't be sorry. Just focus on to get up. Good. Now your little blue traveling bag is still on the same place in the closet?"

Elli couldn't make any sound, so she just moved her head for yes.

"Okay."

"What ... what are you doing, Lisa?"

"I'm packing. That's what I should do a long time ago."

"But—"

"No, Elli. There's no but! I'm doing exactly what you'll be doing for me."

"But—"

"Elli, please. Listen to me at least this time. Please!"

"How is she?"

"Did I wake you up?"

Lisa just slid her exhausted body beside Nick's. It was so good to have him by her side.

"You didn't call. Did you?"

"No. I'm sorry. It was all too emotional. Elli is here, by the way. She'll stay till we'll figure it out what's next. She can't go back there. Not now, that's for sure. You'll understand once you'll read all what's in the box which she found. It's from Danny." Lisa said her last words to Nick almost in whispering voice while falling asleep.

He pulled the cover gently over her shoulders but thought about her last words. After a few turns of his body, Nick got out of the bed and did look up for the mystery box.

It was standing beside Elli's bag on the table. He felt bad to not be able to ask Elli if it's okay to read it. But he knew she'll be okay with it.

Quietly, he got himself a cup of coffee and sat down on the chair in the living room.

He never met Danny, but as he started reading his notes which were out of order, all mixed up in the box, he started to understand little by little Ellie's deep grief.

"So simple Post-it notes but so thoughtful, loving. Looks like a great guy, thought Nick when he finished reading the last one. "Nick, hi. You're up. When did you get up?" Lisa asked while pointing toward the empty mug.

"Hi, my love. Me? I guess since you lay down beside me," Nick said and smiled while he pulled Lisa close to him. "I was trying to fall asleep when you did, but it was impossible." "How come?"

Nick just pointed at the box beside the bag.

"I just couldn't get over your last words about the box and that, and then I'll understand."

"Did you read it?"

"Yes. I hope that's all right. I thought—"

"Yes. Of course it is. Well, I think so."

"Lisa, Danny—I don't know him, but his notes from the past few weeks show like he's, sorry, he was good man."

"You have no idea, Nick. He was intelligent, sporty, with great humor and—"

"Should I be jealous?"

"Oh, stop it. Let me finish! He was caring but in love over the hills for Elli. She was so alive by him."

"I'm sorry not to have a chance to get to know him. So what now, boss?"

"That's the problem. She was the one who always navigates us to the best possible direction. Everything's wrong. Why?"

"We'll find what to do together. Okay?"

Breakfast time went quietly. The first to break the silence was Nick, telling about Easter egg hunting for Katie.

At this moment, all of them were thankful to have her—to be busy to make plans for her and enjoy any activity with her. "Anybody's going to work?" asked Nick, but looking from one to another, he knew the answer. "Looks it's gonna be none but me. Hope you both relax through the day."

"Lisa, hi. Sorry I didn't call earlier. How's everything going?"

"Not good, Nick. Hi. She's completely silent. Moves like robot. Keeps crying."

"Did you try to go out?"

"No chance. She seems to be like in her own world."

"I'm sorry I'm not there. I'll come as soon it'll be possible. Call me if anything."

"I will. I miss you, Nick." Lisa ended the call and headed to the living room to Elli. She was exactly in the same position as she left her while talking to Nick.

"Elli, do you need anything? Extra blanket or tea?" She only shook her head and kept silent.

"I'll call to work. They must be furious by now. Hope we still have the jobs."

After more than twenty minutes on the phone with the main office, Lisa told Elli about what she was told. They were asking Elli for a recommendation from the doctor, if she is still able to work or leave for maternity leave immediately.

"Tomorrow" was the only word Elli was able to get out of herself.

"Tomorrow what, Elli?" Silence.

"Tomorrow we'll go to see your doctor?"

Elli just closed her eyes and slightly moved her head.

"Okay. I'll call to make an appointment."

Chapter 10

"Nick! Nick! Get up! Elli! Nick!"

"What is it, Lisa?" Nick could barely open his eyes to look at Lisa. "Say it! What happened?"

"Elli!" Lisa's face went completely white, all blood drawn away by fear. "She's breathing but no response. I can't wake her up." Lisa's tone of voice was alarming, which made Nick get up right in seconds.

"Where is she?"

"She's still in the bed. Nick, I'm so scared!"

"Call her doctor!"

"There is somebody else at the office. Her doctor is for a few days away. This is not good. This is not good. Not at all. This doctor, he knows nothing about her. Nothing about the babies."

"Lisa, he's a doctor too. I'm sure he was informed about Elli's doctor's patients."

"That's not the point. For him, she'll be just a stranger. A patient. He'll make any decision without any emotions."

"Maybe that's exactly what we need it—what Elli will need right now. I'm sure he'll do the best not to put her or the babies into more danger than needed."

"I hope you're right. I can't lose her or the babies. I'll get insane! Elli, Elli, please wake up. Talk to me, please!" Lisa crushed down beside Elli's bed. Tears were rolling down her cheeks.

"Maybe if I'll shake her hard, she'll open her eyes."

"Lisa, no! Let's wait for the doctor. Please!"

It was like in the bad movie when time did freeze. Lisa felt stomach sick, but she wasn't able to move herself away from Elli.

The doctor was very quiet, precise, and fast.

"Her body is functioning perfectly. More tests will be done in the hospital. I know a little bit about Elli from her doctor, Dr. Raysse. I'm Dr. Mark. Looks like her body was trying to protect itself and just turn off. Babies look all right at this moment. Can you think of something different in last few days what could cause such a reaction? And one more thing, she was holding this Post-it note." The doctor was about to open all crumbled piece of paper and read it when Lisa grabbed it out of his hand. She read it aloud:

"Elli, wish the world have more people like you. I found everything what I could wish for in you. I wasn't afraid to give you my heart at the moment I saw you. I'm lucky to give you my whole heart today, and I'll be the happiest man to do it tomorrow, day after tomorrow …"

"We missed this one. Didn't see that note. She must have held onto it the entire time, Nick." Lisa finished her talk while turning toward Nick with heavy weeping and sobbing. The doctor was looking a little bit out of space, so Nick excused them and tried to shortly describe the situation. Pregnancy of one. Pregnancy of two kids as well as finding the box with Post-it notes from Danny.

"Thank you for filling me in. It was very nice to meet you, but it's time for me to get back to the hospital. So who'll be the person that we can contact?"

"She has no family—family—we are her family."

"No living family or relative?"

"No, just us."

"Okay. I'm sure her doctor has phone numbers on you in the file."

"Yes, she does, but I would like to come with her."

"Get some rest. Give us a time to do some tests, and I'll call you when we'll have something more or when you can come. She'll be in good hands."

While the doctor was talking to them, Elli's body was readied by the ambulance guys for transport to do hospital.

"But—"

"Lisa, listen to the doctor, please. I don't want you to follow Elli."

"I'll be fine. Elli needs me."

"Yes. She does. But not lying in bed next to her. If you continue like this, you might collapse too. Rest a little bit. Eat. We're on the phone. They'll do tests to help them get the clue, to find out what happen and how to help her."

"I know. You're right. I'll have some soup. I don't think I can eat something else."

"You know what, sit down. Here's the blanket." Nick handed a folded fuzzy blanket to Lisa and went to the kitchen to get her some hot soup.

"Nick, what is going on? What the hell is happening? Are we stuck in some horrible circle without a chance to break to get out of it for good? Can't it just go smoothly? How much more are we supposed to take it? I thought I know how Elli felt when she found Danny, but no. I had, and I still have no idea how much she got hurt. We are experiencing just a small amount, small fraction of what she went through. And it's the two of us to deal it with. She was there all alone."

"I don't know what to tell you, Lisa. I felt today too like we're locked in all these things that are happening. All the moments are not bringing anything better, just a lot of loss, sadness. But we've got each other, and we're gonna make it through. Doesn't matter how long it is gonna take. We just have to believe that one day, all the hurt will be just the past and will get us all to the better place in our lives." "What about the box, Nick?"

"Lisa, I think the box belongs to Elli."

"But look what did happen! If it won't be for the box with all those Post-it sticker notes—"

"If it won't be that box, Elli will never know so many beautiful thoughts that Danny has toward her and the possible babies. It's her treasure. We should put the notes nicely in box and save for her."

"But look what it already did to her."

"I know, but she knew at that moment how much she was loved by Danny."

"I don't want her to go through it again."

"She won't."

"You can't know that, Nick. Come on."

"I know. You'll see. Because it's gonna be at different time, different place. She already lived through it."

"She misses him so much. Can you hold me tight, Nick? I need that so much right now. I feel so numb."

"Gladly. I was hoping for it. Is it too tight?"

Chapter 11

"Did anybody call yet from the hospital?" Lisa asked Nick while she was trying to stretch her body a little. They both fell asleep on the sofa. "Can you help me up? I'm sort of stuck."

"I like it this way. I don't really want you to get unstuck of me."

"Funny. Thanks!"

Nick helped Lisa get up and stretched himself, and then he checked his phone. The display was clear.

"Nope. Nobody called yet."

"I'll call them then," said Lisa while searching for the number that they got from the doctor. They should know something by now. Maybe she's up. Nick, I'll go to the hospital. I'm fine now."

"I'll go with you."

"Are you sure? You don't need to go back to work?"

"One hundred percent sure. I'll work later when we'll get back."

"I'm planning to stay there by Elli."

"We'll see, sweetheart. We don't know yet what's going—"

Nick didn't have time to finish the sentence because Lisa signaled him to be quiet. The receptionist just answered the phone call. Nick couldn't hear what Lisa was told, but her face didn't show a much of happiness.

"So?"

"Nothing new yet. She's still asleep," said Lisa while gesturing with her hands. "Her body is functioning perfectly. And the babies look all right. How come they don't know what's going on? With all the technology they have?"

"Maybe Elli is just really recharging. Okay. Let's go there."

"She looks so—"

"Fragile."

Lisa pulled the chair closer to the side of the bed and reached for Ellie's hand.

"Elli, I hope you can hear me. I hope you're all right, and you'll be all right. I miss you so much! Please don't forget who you are. Rest. Recharged, but then please get back to us as you were. We love you. Can you hear me? No. I know you do hear me. You do hear my voice. I should probably try to talk to you as long as it will make you shout at me."

"Lisa, be quiet! Because you'll never tell a person to just shut up. You are too good. Too good and too kind to everybody, so why have you been treated like that?"

"Lisa, try to be positive, optimistic."

"I'm sorry. I got carried away. I know. I know."

The nurse walked into the room and checked Elli's vital function. Few minutes after, Dr. Mark came in. He did pretty much the same thing as the nurse before him and turned to Lisa and Nick.

"Thank you for coming. It's very important for her to hear your voices. For now, I can get you five more minutes. She's getting tired."

"When she will wake up?"

"We still don't know. It's very difficult to be accurate with any exact answers. We're hoping soon."

"What about the babies?"

"They are both all right. If anything, we're ready to get them to this world by C-section anytime. I'll let you be with her alone for five more minutes, but then, please, stop at my office on your way out. We'll talk more there."

"Thank you, doctor. We will."

"Why you were so hard on that doctor? He seems to me as he is doing his best."

"I don't know him. For the whole time, Elli was going to Dr. Raysse. Now all of a sudden, close to the birth of the babies, she needs her doctor, but stranger, he doesn't know her."

"He told us in the beginning. But good thing is, he was informed by Dr. Raysse. And he really makes the impression of being professional with each patient."

"And that's the thing. She isn't just patient. She's our Elli who we're talking about, with two kids almost ready to come out."

"Lisa, we're here. They'll do their best. Maybe Dr. Raysse will return sooner."

"We'll see. It's hard. That's nothing like she has a cold. Then I'll know what to do. I'll know how to help her, how long it's gonna last. In this case, I don't know about you, but I don't know more now after the talk with Dr. Mark, as I did before. We figured it out already and the cause of it. We didn't get an answer for how long it might last. There's really no medicine for her to take to cure her faster. What we were told now? Only that our visits and talking and massaging her lying body will help her keep in better condition than if we won't make time to come. And I guess that's nothing new to both of us."

"Lisa, please be patient. That's all what she and the doctor need right now. They won't let her just lay around. We'll be here as often as we can. Now it's time to go back home. They'll not let you to be with her right now. Plus we have stuff to do."

"I don't care. I can sit in the hallway. What stuff?"

"Happy I can remind you! We need to get buy those cribs that Elli mentioned, since you girls didn't make it on time to do store. Otherwise, I have no idea where the babies will sleep. Second, I would like to spend more time by looking up some properties. Just on PC now, till we make down to a few which we will go to see in person. Which reminds me, we need to get that box with Post-it nicely, put it together, and get it back to her apartment."

"Why? If it wasn't for that box, she'll be here with us."

"We did already talk about it. It was important, very important to her as to the babies will be one day. You'll see. They'll look for the answers to the questions, and that will help them understand. It'll let them know how much they were wanted and loved by both of them. Lisa, once she'll wake up, she'll be stronger than she was ever before."

"But no one knows if she'll wake up. And then what kind of damage she might have."

"Shhh. Come here. It'll be all right. Now we need to keep strong and focus on what we just talked about— little things which we're able to do for her and babies. Done with crying?"

"Yes. I'm ready."

"That's my girl. That's the woman that I fell for."

Chapter 12

"Okay. So we've got cribs. That was easy since she already had an idea which one she does like. Are you sure she was all right to put them together here?"

"I think so. She won't be able to go back to her apartment and take care of the babies on her own. And if you'll move in, you all won't be able to move happily by each other. So till we'll find something more suitable, this seems to be the best choice."

"What now?"

"Wasn't that enough for you today?"

"No."

"Don't scare me. You look like you have strength to do all what I mentioned at once."

"Yes. Why not?"

"All right, we can try put the box back together."

"You know what? Can we leave the box for some other time. I … I … I really don't … I'm not ready for it."

"So properties?"

"Yes."

"Let's get something to eat and something to drink to bed, and we can work on that."

"Sounds good to me."

"Nick!"

"It's so good to see you smile. I missed that a lot." For a moment, they put everything on the side.

"Did you have a chance to go to the hospital, Lisa?"

"Yes. Today, I went there over my lunch break."

"Any changes?"

"Nothing. All seems to be the same. But Dr. Mark was there before me. He didn't realize right away that I was there. It was …"

"What?"

"I don't know."

"Something's wrong?"

"No. Not at all. He was sitting closer to her. He ran his fingertips through Elli's hair to make them better, and while holding her hand, he opened the book and continued reading. So I made a noise like I just came, and I pretended I just saw him."

"Oh, I mean, isn't that what you wanted him to do? Not to just take Elli as patient who belongs to another doctor? Her doctor, Dr. Raysse, is still not back."

"No. But Dr. Mark said she did call him and ask about Elli."

"Good. She's in good hands, Lisa."

"Yeah. I guess. But isn't it too much?"

"I think she's in good hands of two doctors who care about her."

"We should keep an eye on him and maybe try not to go there at the same time so we'll cover more time. You know what I mean? No schedule, so they won't know when we'll be there as well."

"I have no problem with that, but I think you're overreacting. I'll better not even imagine what you'll tell me, when I'll be turning her and giving her massage so she'll have easier movements when she'll ready to wake up."

"Silly."

"Nick, are you busy? Can you talk?"

"Hi. I have a few minutes' time. What's going on?"

"I saw him."

"You saw who?"

"I saw Dr. Mark again by her. He did hold her hand and was telling some stories."

"Lisa, that's fine. We can't be there all the time. And if for Elli, this is making easier passed the time—"

"Yeah, but—"

"But what? Can't you let it go?"

"Okay."

Chapter 13

"How's my favorite, Dr. Mark?"

"Hi, Sue. Dr. Raysse. How's your vacation going?"

"Too fast, but I miss you. Thanks for taking over me while I'm gone."

"So you're enjoying yourself?"

"Yes. All is so nice here. So how're the patients?"

Dr. Mark gave Dr. Raysse fast update on everyone, except Elli.

"You forgot about Elli. Is something—"

"No. I didn't," said Dr. Mark, not even letting Dr. Raysse finish the sentence.

"Is something wrong? How is she doing? Anything new? If yes, why nobody didn't inform me about it?"

"No. Nothing's new. She's doing okay. Maybe just her heartbeat did speed up a little because of the pressure of the babies. Maybe in two to three days, we'll need to get them out."

"Do you need me to come back now, or you'll handle it okay?"

"I'm okay. They're in good position, so there shouldn't be any complications with C-section. She's so ... fragile."

"Are you okay?"

"Yes. Why?"

"You sound nothing like yourself at all."

"Why. No. I'm okay. Maybe a little bit tired. That's all."

"Okay. If you say so. Call me if anything."

"I will."

"Dr. Mark, I think you should go to see Elli."

"What's going on?"

"All things are showing we should go for C-section."

"I was hoping they'll wait few more days, but they seem to be strong enough. Okay then. Let's get everything ready. Did you contact everyone from the surgery team?"

"Yes. They're getting ready."

"All right. I'll be right there too."

The nurse disappeared behind the not fully closed door. He could hear voices from the hallway. He saw his own reflection in the old mirror hanging above the sink. He made one step closer. His face was turning terribly white. All he was able to do, while splashing cold running water all over his face, was thinking about Elli and wishing all of three of them will be all right after the surgery.

"Dr. Mark, are you alright?"

"Yes. Why?"

"You look ... nothing. Everyone is ready."

"Good. Let's get started."

Chapter 14

"Nick! Nick! Elli's babies are born! All of them are okay. I'm on my way to the hospital."

"That's so exciting. I'm on my way. I was supposed to pick up Katie, but it will be better if I'll pick her up after."

"I think so. All will settle down when she'll visit."

"You're right."

"See you soon."

"I can't wait."

When Nick arrived to the hospital, he was lucky to talk right away to Dr. Mark. He was still looking too pale but happy to Nick. He led him straight to the room where the newborns were.

"Since they both were big and vital enough, we do not worry about them. In few days, I'm sure we'll see a significant change in their growth. They still have no names. They should have before they'll leave the hospital, but …"

"They're both beautiful. Aren't babies so amazing?"

"These two for sure. Just like their mom."

"Anything new about Elli?"

"She is stabilized right now. Labor was too exhausting for her body. But nothing else changed. I'll take you to her. I'm going to check up on her anyway. Lisa is by her right now."

"Did she see the babies?"

"Yes. She loves them just like the rest of us," said Dr. Mark to Nick, and finally his face was regaining back healthy color.

"Thank you, doctor."

"Gladly."

"Does Elli's doctor, Dr. Raysse, know ..."

"She knows everything. She was calling multiple times in the past few days."

"What a vacation for a doctor, right?"

"That's okay. We love it. Every job has something. But it feels great to bring to life new human being—in our case, two."

"Dr. Mark, can I ask you something?"

"Go ahead. You already started."

"You've spend lots of time by Elli. Please don't take me wrong. We do appreciate everyone's effort toward Elli. She's such a sweetheart. Several months were just ..."

"I know. I've heard a little from Dr. Sue Raysse and you."

"Why?"

"Why what?"

"Why do you spend so much time by Elli?"

"I don't know. It just felt so peaceful. I mean she looked more peaceful when I or someone else was by her. I thought once I saw her smile a little, but that might be just me wishing too hard for it—for any reactions from her."

"I'm sorry. I didn't mean to ..."

"That's okay. She's so lucky to have you both. You and Lisa." "And Katie."

"Yes. Sorry. Katie too. She loves her very much. I saw that. It's amazing."

When Nick and Dr. Mark arrived to Elli's room, Lisa was in tears sitting quietly beside Elli. Dr. Mark checked all Elli's functions. Nick hugged Lisa and asked her gently what's going on.

"Nothing, Nick. And that's the problem. I want her to get off that stupid sleeping mode. I want her to get up and go see her little girl and boy. She rested already enough. I don't want her to miss a thing. And I miss her too."

"Lisa, come. Let's go outside. Elli needs to regain her strength after labor. Come and see the babies. Come, please. Dr. Mark might be here for a short time. She won't be alone."

"Yes. I'll be here for a while."

"Okay. I'm sorry. I'm so sorry. I love you, Elli. I'll be back in a little. Then I'll tell you how the babies are doing."

"Come on, Lisa."

"I'm coming!"

When the door closed behind them, Nick spoke gently to Lisa about Elli's kids and also about his approach to Dr. Mark about spending great amount of time by Elli.

"What did he say to you?"

"Not really much. He pretty much sounded as a doctor to me. But I might be wrong. His face was becoming softer each time he talks about her."

"I'm telling you, it isn't a regular patient-doctor relationship. Something is different."

"Hey. What was happening to you few minutes ago by Elli?"

"I know. I'm sorry for it. I just felt so helpless. It seems to me like forever. I almost grab her shoulders to shake her but glad you both came in. Nick, I'm losing my beliefs. I was hoping after few days, she'll be up. I never thought about that possibility of babies being born and her still asleep."

"I know. It's tough. But I still believe she'll be all right. Give her more time, Lisa. Please."

"But the babies—"

"They are fine. They've got us. They're not lonely."

"Nurse, excuse me. Hi. I was stopping by to see Elli's babies, but …"

"Dr. Mark took them to her."

"He took them to Elli?"

"Yes."

"Is there something new about Elli? Nobody did give us a call."

"No. Not that I know."

"So why Dr. Mark took the babies to her?"

"Oh. I thought you knew."

"I know what?"

"Dr. Mark is doing so every day. He feeds them there and changes them while talking to her."

"Is Dr. Mark the same way with other patients?"

"Well, putting this way, no. But none of them did get the twins while in coma."

"Understand. It's all so difficult. I apologize. I didn't mean to …"

"Dr. Mark is a nice man. He really loves his job. He's brokenhearted if anything goes wrong."

"Okay. I'm sorry for asking."

"Not a problem."

"Thanks."

"Nick, are you sure there's nothing else going on on the side of Dr. Mark?"

"Why?"

"When I was visiting Elli today, I was going to stop by the twins first. As usual. Then I felt I'll have the rest of the time for Elli."

"How is she?"

"She's good."

"And how are the twins? Katie can't wait to go see them again."

"They're fine too. Do you really need to interrupt me, or will you let me, please, finish?"

"Sorry. Go ahead."

"So ..."

"But I'm glad they're fine."

"Nick!"

"What? I'm just saying I'm glad all of them are fine, and now I'm quiet, and I'm all ears for you."

"Thank you. Finally. So today, I found out Dr. Mark is taking the twins every day to Elli's room, and he spends a lot of time there."

"You just can't drop off that thing, can't you?"

"I can't. I really believe that's not normal."

"What do you want to do about it?"

"I don't know."

"Lisa. I really believe you should let it go. We should be all just thankful she, I mean, the three of them are in such good hands. If it won't be him, and at this point, it doesn't really matter what his intentions are. Am I right? She'll be alone. The twins will be alone till we will be able to get to them. Is that what you want?"

"No."

"Then, please, let it go. Don't forget there are always nurses around."

"Maybe you're right."

"In this, I am. Lisa, please, let go of it."

"Mark, hi. Can I talk to you?"

"Sure, Dr. Raysse."

"Oh, come on. Stop with that. Nobody is around."

"Do you need something?"

"Mark, what's going on? You're completely avoiding me since my return from vacation."

"I have just been busy."

"Don't start like that. You're talking to me. Sue. For how long we know each other?"

"For a while."

"So what's going on? And straight. That's how we always were with each other."

"I know. I'm sorry, Sue. I have no idea what's happening. Something is drowning me every day to go see Elli and the twins. I feel so happy and peaceful when I'm with them."

"Mark, she's your patient and—"

"No, she's not. She's your patient, not mine. Technically."

"But you delivered her babies."

"But she's not my patient officially."

"I'm not sure about how they can classify it."

"You know what, Sue, I don't really care at this point. I did first and last for this hospital for years. Life passes by."

"What about us? Did we just pass by as the life in the hospital?"

"Sue, I don't know what I can say. It's just different. Strong."

"You have not even a clue what's gonna happen next. Will she wake up? Will there be any reconcilable damage? And if not, what will she feel toward you? It's only you and the people around who'll remember all what happened before her wakingup time. To her, you'll be just a stranger. The doctor."

"Maybe she'll remember something. Who knows? Maybe she'll remember my voice." "Most likely, none of it."

"You don't know. Nobody knows."

"We can have our own kid. I'm ready."

"Sue, I'm sorry. I can't. I feel I belong to them."

"Yeah. I'm sorry too. If you ever need something, you know where I am."

"Sue? Thank you. You're the best."

"Best maybe, but not the one. Evidently. Be careful."

Chapter 15

"Nick, I can't believe it. We did it! Katie is so happy to have her own room."

"I know!"

"This is our home. Past is solved. You're officially divorced, and we do both come here, home. No more multiple places. Isn't that amazing?"

"No. You're amazing to me, Lisa. We've been through a lot but got closer to each other than we were when we started. Will you marry me?"

"Nick, are you insane?"

"That's great! I'm asking you to marry me, and your answer to it is that I'm insane."

"What do you expect me to say? You've just got divorced.

You're only a few days out of marriage."

"But I feel this way for you as long as I can remember."

"And we can't plan to get married when Elli is still in the hospital."

"And?"

"And stop it."

"You don't love me?"

"I do."

"So?"

"So nothing."

"Are you scared? You are scared!"

"No, I'm not. I'm not scared."

"So?"

"So stop, Nick. We do have each other. Isn't that the most what we can have?"

"No. It's not. You can be my wife, and I can be your husband."

"Nick, please."

"Okay. I'll give you break, Lisa, but I'll ask you again. Probably tomorrow."

"You're so hilarious. I love you."

Chapter 16

"Lisa, come to the hospital please."

"What's going on, Nick?"

"It's Elli."

Lisa almost dropped the phone from her hand. She stood speechless trying to catch the air.

"Lisa?"

"Yes. I'm listening."

"Elli woke up. She is—" Nick wasn't able to even really start explaining to Lisa what's going on when she interrupted him.

"I'm on my way, Nick. I'll be right there. Stay by her, please!" "I will—if they won't ask me to leave."

However, Lisa didn't hear that part at all. She hung up as soon as she heard Elli woke up and let Nick know she's on the way. She was glad at least Nick was there by Elli. She wanted to have her closest friend back. Nick was great. But he wasn't Elli. She missed her so much. Sometimes she was mad at her to be just lying there with such a peace on her face while the babies were making through their first days of life, while they did purchase places for all of them, while there was so much that she was just talking to her and hoping she can hear her voice and catch all important or not so important thing and hoping something from it will pull her back to the real world. It was becoming frustrating. Lisa felt sometimes the urge to just grab her and shake her as strong as possible to end that ridiculous sleep. But she knew it won't do any good. Evidently, being patient wasn't her strongest part. That's why she needed Elli so much to get back. She was the most patient one. Lisa didn't realize when she got to the hospital. It was a very tense feeling. She didn't know what to expect. Will Elli be as before? Will she recognize her? Or is she gonna be stranger lying in the bed in front of her?

"Well, whatever it's gonna be, I'm not gonna let you forget about us. Wanted or not, you'll remember us at some point. You have to, Elli!"

"Nick! Hi! How is she?"

"Hi. Slow down! She seems to be okay so far. They are still doing testing."

"Can we go in? Can I see her?"

"Let's go see the twins first. That will put you to the happy, slow mode. Then we'll go see if they're done so we can go in."

"Okay. But only for a short moment. She's up already for a while. It took me forever to get here. Even tell you the truth, Nick, I have no idea how I got in here."

"Are you trying to be apologizing for any ticket coming in the mail?"

"Funny! But if something will come, I won't be surprised. I just drove and drove. I was trying to think about Elli and—"

"Did I cross your mind?"

"Nick!"

"What?"

"Come on!"

"What? I'm just curious. So I'm asking. Because I was thinking about you a lot."

By that time, they entered the room where the twins were peacefully asleep.

"Aren't they so cute? And peaceful?"

"You knew they're asleep now. Didn't you, Nick?"

"How did you know?"

"Because you'll be not taking me here if they're all hungry, dirty, crying. Simple. Isn't it?"

"Yes. I knew. I was here till our phone call."

"So you did all the hard work while I was at home."

"No problem. Who knows if I'll be able to get you out of the hospital at all, since Elli is up."

"Can we go see Elli now?"

"Few more minutes, Lisa."

"Nick! You are torturing me."

"Nope. I'm trying to take time. They're not calling yet. So …"

"Okay. Few more minutes. But then straight to Elli. I can't believe I agreed to that!"

"Good girl," Nick said and smiled at Lisa.

Nick knew she'll relaxed by the time she'll be able to go see Elli. Good thing about the twins was that no matter how the day was exhausting and tiring, one of them was for sure to make it all good. Nick thought while he was looking at Lisa's face while she enjoyed the view of the twins both sleeping. But he sensed something was out of balance with Lisa. And he didn't think that it has anything to do with Elli. He decided to ask Lisa about that later. At this moment, he also enjoyed just being there with all of them. He felt immediately recharged, ready for the next obstacle, blessed to have so many people to live for. Suddenly, Nick felt his phone vibrating, so he stepped out to the hallway. It was the call that they were waiting for. He took a deep breath till he answered the call.

"Lisa. Lisa," said Nick, lowering his voice.

"Nick, where did you disappear? Elli?"

"Yes. I felt my phone vibrating, so I stepped out to the hallway. They called that they are done for now with the testing so we can come see her."

"Oh, Nick," said Lisa while her eyes filled up with the tears.

"It's gonna be okay, Lisa. Let's go. That's what we were waiting for. It's better to face whatever it is than stay here paralyzed and wonder."

"I'm ready. Let's go."

Before entering Elli's room, they stopped to chat with the doctor.

"All of Elli's functions seem all right. She knows who she is. She recognizes where she is. She doesn't know what happened. She did ask about the babies and you— which is good. But she's very weak, so I'll let you go in only for ten minutes max. She needs to get rest."

"Thank you, Dr. Sue," said both of them at once while Lisa was already opening the door. She ran like a little girl to Elli's bed, smiled at her through the tears, and gently hugged her.

Nick walked slowly closer and said, "Hi, Elli. Glad you're awake!"

All smiled. They talked for a short time, mostly about the babies and Katie, when the doctor appeared in the door.

"I'm very sorry to interrupt you, but she really needs to get some rest."

"He's not sorry at all," said Lisa to Elli with a whispering voice. That's what he does the entire time. He's like your guardian."

Elli seemed extremely tired, but she couldn't help but giggle. When the three of them stepped out, Nick didn't wait for Dr. Mark to walk away but asked Lisa what she whispered. She looked at Dr. Mark and repeated exactly what she said to Elli without moving her eyes from Dr. Mark.

Nick felt frozen for a second and rolled his eyes while wishing not to ask her about that right away, but it was too late. All was out. Dr. Mark cleared his throat and seemed, for a second, his tired face showed signs of blush. They all were looking at him in expectation for more reaction. He knew Lisa won't let go of it and let them just dismiss. So he cleared his throat once more and said in an easy tone as possible in this situation, "I'm glad Elli is doing well, and you all had a great time, but it's time to give her space and time to recover. I'm happy I can help with that." While talking, his voice got more professional; and before Lisa could make any other comment, he opened the door and made the gesture toward her to walk out of the room. For his and Nick's relief as well, she did!

"Thank you, Dr. Mark, for everything," Nick said and pulled Lisa by her elbow closer to him.

"You're welcome. Tomorrow, we will repeat all the tests. Hopefully, no changes will occur overnight. If not, we will try to make the best decision for Elli about the physical procedures followed by rehabilitation exercises as an outpatient. It'll be just approximately. We'll adjusted by her progress."

"Thank you, doctor. When can we come tomorrow?"

"Pretty much anytime. I think she'll progress better when you'll be here."

"No doubt about it!" Lisa said while she stretched her hand toward Dr. Mark, and all of them said goodbye.

"What was that?"

"What?"

"You know exactly what I meant, Lisa! First, whispering to Elli and then saying aloud what you said to Dr. Mark."

"I'm just trying to figure out what he's up to."

"Are you serious?"

"Deadly."

"Why? Who cares about his intention anyway? I think at this point we should be endlessly thankful for everybody's attention. Good attention. Let's not forget about that—to help Elli or even just to be around her."

"I guess. All right. You're right, Nick! But she went through so much, and I'll not let—not even Dr. Mark— get her down."

"I know. But I think you should ease up on him. That's all."

They both walked in silence toward the car. The weather was very nice. Nick looked shortly at Lisa while opening the door. She seemed to be focused, or what was it? It was exactly the same look on her face while they're both visiting the twins before going to see Elli. They closed the car doors at the same time, but Nick didn't start the car. After a while, Lisa realized they're still at the same spot. She turned her head toward Nick that was looking at her.

"Hey. Why we're not going?" asked Lisa.

"I'm not sure if I should ask you now or just get us home and ask you then."

"I guess you should just ask now since you started."

"Would you like to go for smoothie?"

"Nick!"

"Yes?"

"What is it? What are you going to asked me? And yes to a smoothie," Lisa said and gave Nick a smile with a silly wink.

Nick leaned toward her and kissed her happily, with his hand close, putting away the hair that kept coming between them. He closed his eyes after their kiss and looked into Lisa's eyes. Then he whispered question that he was starting to guess what the answer will be: "What were you thinking about when we were by the twins today before we went to see Elli?"

Lisa's face turned for a second the same way as Nick caught a glimpse of it in the twins' room as well as when they walked to the car. Then she blushed, but she remained silent. He put his forehead on hers and asked her with a bit of hoarse voice, "Were you thinking about us? Were you … were you thinking about us having a baby? To be a family?"

Lisa wasn't able to make a sound. He wasn't going to move the car, not even his look away from her till he'll get the answer from her.

"Yes, Nick. I was. But …" She hung her head a little.

Nick lifted her chin up till their eyes met again. "But what?"

"But it's always something happening. We're so busy. Work. Katie. Twins. Elli. Now townhouses."

Nick smiled with relief. "Come closer, Lisa." He pulled her as close as it was possible in the car. "We will never be too busy to have our own kid. I'm happy you feel the same way. I didn't want to seem like I'm rushing. Glad you didn't think I'm crazy when I gave you the ring. But I did wish you'll want it as much as I do."

"But, Nick, there is so much going on …"

"Shhh, Lisa. There will always be something going on. That doesn't mean we will stop living, stop dreaming, stop wanting."

"But what about Katie?"

"What about her?"

"I love her. I don't want to hurt her. She's a great girl. She trusts us."

"We will show her she'll still have the same place in our hearts. She'll still have her own room in our house. She'll have our attention as till now."

"Can we manage through all this? With the twins coming home? Elli, we still don't know yet exactly how everything will go."

"I know, Lisa. Too many but no clear answers to too many questions. But …" At that moment, both of them laughed. "But that's life, Lisa. And we know what we want, but what's more important, we know what we have in each other."

"Sue. Hi. What time is it?"

"It's 6:00 a.m. What time did you get here?"

"I actually didn't leave."

"What? Why? Are you trying to kill yourself? Go home. Get good sleep. Shower. When was last time you did eat?"

"Too many questions at once, Dr. Raysse."

"Evidently, they need to be asked! You're going to scare away all the patients. You look horrible."

"Thanks. You look great as usual."

"But that's not enough, unfortunately," said Sue quietly.

Dr. Mark raised himself off the chair quietly, and without any comments to Sue's last words, he gave her short report about higher fever that Elli developed in the late hour the evening before, so he stayed to make sure it was only small inflammation. He knew Elli's body is still very weak, and anything like this might put her in danger.

"Lisa, since when are you reading books like this?"

"Hi, Elli. How are you? I was told you had fever last night."

"Hi, Lisa. Yes. But I feel okay now. Just a little bit sweaty. I can't wait to get shower. Being more accurate, I can't wait to get shower at home!"

"So you better cool down yourself, otherwise, they'll never let you leave the hospital. Especially the owner of this book!"
"Oh, book. Do you know to whom the book belongs? When I woke up, it was lying on the chair."

"I'm pretty sure about to whom the book belongs. To your guardian angel."

Elli gave Lisa a little bit of confused look when she, all of a sudden, remembered the situation between Dr. Mark and Lisa.

"It's Dr. Mark's?"

"Bingo. My smart girl is back," Lisa said, and they both giggled. "I missed that! I missed you, Elli, so much! Did you see the twins today? I went straight to you."

"Not yet. They just finished the morning routine. But I can't wait to see them. I know you all are taking good care of them, but I feel I'm failing on them as a mom."

"You have to stop to feel this way. You're a great mom. Just right now, you need to get yourself to a better shape so you'll be able to take care of them. So back to the book. Evidently, you had a visitor last night."

"Visitor? Oh! Silly. As you already found out, I didn't even know to whom the book belongs. Why is it so important to you?"

"Well, I'm trying to figure out the meaning of it. The meaning of it all. Seems to me, Dr. Mark is really spending enormous time with you. I think much more than with any other patient."

"Maybe it's just your feeling. I'm sure he's a great doctor, and he does take care of his other patients as well."

"I'm not saying he's not. It's just … it's just that my instinct is telling me something, and you know me. I just have to figure it out."

"There's one thing, which is weird. He feels so familiar. As I know him for years."

"Ha! There you go!"

Elli closed her eyes for a moment.

"Are you okay, Elli? Or should I call for help?"

"I'm okay. Just getting tired very fast. But don't worry about it. Tell me about all of you, about work, etc. What all did I miss?"

Lisa started talking about the world outside while giving a gentle massage to Elli's hands. They both turned their heads toward the door that got open all of a sudden. Dr. Mark stepped into the room with Elli's babies pushed in the cart in front of him.

"Hello, Elli. Hello, Lisa."

"Hello, Dr. Mark."

"Hello. Oh my god. Now I'm not so sure which one of you is the patient!" said Lisa while staring at Dr. Mark. He looked like he slept in his doctor's coat, if he even slept. His hair looked as he made his best in few seconds in the bathroom with a little help of water.

"They're awake, changed, and fed. But, Elli, enjoy them but only for a few minutes, okay? We don't want you to get overtired and repeat the fever," said Dr. Mark, completely ignoring Lisa's comments. He knew very well, not to mention the previous comment from Dr. Sue, how he looked. But he wanted to see Elli once more after seeing his patients, and he wanted to see her with the twins together. It didn't cross his mind that Lisa will be already there. But he thought it was worth to get through any of Lisa's comments to see Elli, to see her happy. He felt drowned to keep going to see her and the twins as well.

When the doors closed behind him, Lisa commented, "See?"

"What?"

"Come on, Elli. He is lighting up like Christmas tree when he's around you and the babies."

"I'm sure he's like that by his other patients as well!"

"I won't be so sure about that. Because all of you three, I don't think he have much time for those others. Just saying. By the way, the twins are great! Let me know when you'll be ready for picking the names for them. You still have a little help with that from all of us in a little envelope in the nightstand drawer. I'll go see the twins, how they are doing back there, and then I'll come back. Try to take a nap. Elli, I'm so happy you're okay," said Lisa with relief in her voice. "I see the book—he didn't take it. He'll be back," Lisa said and left with a silly smile on her face.

Chapter 17

Dr. Mark sped up on his motorcycle between the cars to get himself faster to bed. He felt like he should just stay at the hospital to get some sleep, but he had to admit he looked terrible, and he won't function much longer like that. He just felt so good, so energized when he was near Elli or the twins but so breathless, speechless as well; but till Elli was in coma, that wasn't a problem. Now he knew he have to put himself together and not let it show. Even when he just helped Sue with Elli as her patient, he did deliver the twins. It bothered him so much. He felt helpless. He just knew he didn't feel anything like this by any other from his short- or long-term relationships. Something happened that he couldn't make sense of. And since Elli woke up, these feelings got much stronger. He felt chills just to hear her voice. She made him feel so good. When she was asleep, it was so nice to fit her hand into his. Her hands were small, cold when his were warm and warm when his were cold. He wasn't afraid of the judgment from people around, but he knew what she went through, and he didn't know what to do to not ruin anything that might be real.

No. He wasn't afraid. He was scared not to see her smile, not to see the twins. Thinking about everything over and over again, he stepped to take a fast shower, and then he fixed himself fast rice with chicken and threw himself to the bed. The last thing that he thought was wishing to have Elli by his side—to hold her in his arms. Then he drifted away.

Several hours later, he woke up very hungry and alone. He got himself eggs, the only thing left, that was in edible condition.

He grabbed the phone and dialed Sue's number. He could tell the difference in her voice, excited in the beginning to hear him and disappointed after getting the question about Elli and the twins. She was still hoping. She didn't let go—that it might work between them. He felt sad. He knew Sue is nice, but his heartbeat was going crazy just by the thought of Elli.

Elli was getting stronger every day. Higher fever did repeat two more times when she overworked herself. She just wanted so badly to be again independent—walk on her own, take shower on her own, hold her babies, and be able to take care of them.

Lisa and Nick were still taking turns in visits. Katie and some people from work came as well.

She progressed very well, so it was time, by the view of Dr. Sue Raysse, to let Elli go home and schedule the outpatient visit for her and the babies as well. But before they were able to go home, Elli was in charge to make the final decision about the twin's names. She knew all the names in the envelope, but all of a sudden, she couldn't help, and she named them Daniela and Mark. She thanked Dr. Raysse and went toward Nick's car, accompanied by Lisa, when in the entrance, they met Dr. Mark.

His eyes were happy but showed hint of sadness to see them about to leave.

"Hello, Dr. Mark."

"Hello, Elli. I see you all are leaving us."

"Hello," said Lisa. "It was about time."

"Well, I … I wish you the best, and I hope you'll all visit us soon."

"Doctor?" called Elli with one foot out of the door.

"Yes, Elli?"

"Thank you, and hope it's okay I named my son after you."

He could feel his pulse going for a race, faster and faster. It took him lots of effort to keep himself calm as much as possible and to answer to her.

"It's an honor for me, Elli. Thank you."

He didn't need to say more because Elli just smiled and stepped out of the hospital building.

Dr. Mark was standing, still following her by his look to get with her twins and friends to the car till they completely disappeared from his view. He stood there, passed by many people entering and exiting the hospital.

"Mark! Mark, hi."

"Hi, Sue. How are you?"

"I'm okay. How about you?"

"I'm … I'm great. She named her son Mark."

She smiled at him. She was hurt, but she knew he will never feel about her what he feels for Elli.

"Yes, she did. I think it's a good sign but a long run to get to the happy ending. Plus on the top, you need to get through her bodyguard Lisa."

They both smiled at each other.

"But I guess it's worth it. I wish you the best with it," Sue said and exited the building as fast as she could to not let him or any patients see her tears.

Mark felt too happy, too good to pay attention to Sue; he couldn't get over it that Elli named her son after him. For the rest of his shift, he couldn't hide the smile.

Chapter 18

Days were passing by, and Mark was missing to see Elli and the twins. He knew he missed their visit, so he asked Dr. Sue to let him know about their next appointment and not to miss them again.

He found himself getting on his motorcycle to go for a ride and look for her face. He wished to at least catch the glimpse of her, just to see her and to know they're okay.

Elli was touched by all the effort of Nick and Lisa, so she couldn't have the heart to turn them down. With their help, she went back to Danny's and her place. She picked her things piece by piece. She made sure nothing was left behind and moved all belongings to their new home, the townhouse that Nick with Lisa picked. She felt pain. She felt scared, very afraid. But she knew she needed to do that change. Elli had two great reasons to make that big step, to start to make everything better step by step. Now she understood Danny will be with them forever. The look at the asleep twins was taking the hurt away.

But something surprised her. She missed one voice, the voice so comforting that was filling up the hole inside. She got lost in thoughts.

Katie ran toward her. "Elli, Elli," she shouted from the doorway in sort of mix of quiet and high voice and full of excitement. "Guess who I met outside of the store? Guess who? Give a try! Please. Please. Please!"

"Pssst," said Elli while closing the door quietly behind her where the twins were falling asleep.

"I don't know, but I have the feeling you're going to tell me," said Elli while smiling at Katie and leading her toward the kitchen.

"Would you like to get crazy good smoothie and cookie?"

"First, try to guess, please."

"Okay. Any hints for me? My brain is a little bit slow today."

Katie started to giggle. "Okay. One. One hint. It is someone who is very important for all of us."

"Hmm. That sounds interesting. You made me curious."

"So any guess, Elli?"

"What about one more hint, Katie?"

"Come on, Elli. Okay, his name starts with letter M."

All of a sudden, Elli swallowed hard. She felt as if she got all of a sudden dizzy. She was about to tell her guess aloud when Katie lost the patience, and while disappearing, Elli only caught her saying that she took him there to come to see them all.

All of a sudden, Elli was looking straight at Mark. Dr. Mark was standing in the door speechless, exactly as Elli was. His heart was pounding fast, and he was scared they can hear how loud it is.

Katie realized nobody was saying a word, so she made fun of them in the form of introducing them to each other. "Elli, this is Mark. Mark this is Elli." And without waiting for Elli's confirmation, she pulled Mark by his sleeve while explaining that the twins were just falling asleep. She quietly opened the door. Mark followed her, passing Elli with a short smile, while Elli rolled her eyes.

Mark felt so happy, as he didn't since Elli left the hospital with the twins. He was looking at the twins and at Elli. Mark realized he didn't say a word. After stepping quietly out with Katie from the twins' room, he said, "Hi."

"Hi, Mark. I mean Dr. Mark," Elli corrected herself.

"I think Mark is just fine," said Mark with a smile on his face. "I'm gonna call Dad and Lisa! They'll be happy to see you!"

Before they could do or say anything, Katie disappeared in the door.

"Hi." "Hi."

"How are you doing?"

"I think we are doing our best. What we—"

Elli didn't even finish because Katie appeared with Nick and Lisa. Elli just showed them all to move quietly to the kitchen, not to wake up babies. They all sat around the small table that she kept from Danny's and her place. They fit just fine since none of them needed to keep bigger distance from each other.

The twins took a great nap, so nobody realized it got already dark outside. Mark stood up and apologized that he stayed for so long. He never checked the time. Not at once. He felt great to see them and to be by all of them. Elli walked him to the door where Katie couldn't be missing.

"Mark, are you busy on Fourth of July? If not, come. We'll be just doing barbecue and enjoying the firework from the backyard. The neighbors told us they can see it very well from here."

"Katie!" said Nick. "Mark, if you won't have anything more interesting or if you didn't plan something already, we'll be happy to have you here to celebrate with us."

Elli and Lisa just exchanged looks. They couldn't believe what is just happening.

"I'll come gladly. I don't have any plans made."

"Yay," said Katie happily. "That'll be fun!"

"All right, Katie, time to go for you as well. We need to get you to your mom."

"Oh, Daddy."

"It's okay. You'll be back soon. Say bye to everybody. Lisa, are you coming with us?"

"Okay. Sure. Bye, Mark. It was great to see you. We'll be back soon, Elli."

"See you then. Bye, Katie. I love you."

Nick, with Lisa and Katie, drove away and left Mark and Elli alone standing in the hallway.

"That was … very dynamic," said Mark, and both of them laughed.

"Thank you for a very nice time and invitation for the Fourth of July. I'll come really gladly. But if that doesn't work for you, I'll understand."

"No. Not at all. Seems like everyone is enjoying your company. And if you would like to bring someone along, that person is invited as well," said Elli by looking at Mark and watching for his reaction.

"No. I don't have anybody to come with, so if boring me will be okay, will be enough, then I'm happy."

"Of course. And you're not boring, but I'm sure you know that."

"So see you then, Elli."

"Yes. Bye, Mark."

They smiled at each other, and Mark turned away. While taking the stairs down, Elli said, "I missed your voice."

Mark stopped walking down the stairs. For a moment, he had to close his eyes. He felt that incredibly nice chill get through his body. Elli realized she said her thoughts aloud. She covered her mouth with her left hand. But it was too late. Her thoughts were now words that were between her and Mark.

Mark didn't know how, but all of a sudden, he was back upstairs by Elli, holding her face in his hands and getting her hair off her face. "And I missed you, Elli. I'll see you on fourth." He smiled at her and went to his motorcycle.

"Drive carefully," said Elli quietly while watching him taking off the driveway. He couldn't hear that. She said that too quietly, and his motorcycle was loud, louder than her voice, louder than his thoughts. His brain was so busy to process what just happened. He wasn't sure what's next, but he was so happy— thankful for Katie that she pulled him in. Closer to Elli. And Lisa did give him a break. Finally! The breeze hit his face— that was, when he grinned while he realized he didn't put his helmet on.

"Lisa, I need to talk to you!" Elli texted shortly after Mark disappeared in the distance on his motorcycle. She stood in the doorway frozen for a minute, and then she covered her mouth with her left hand while her mind was coming to sense to what just happened. She panicked and went back inside the townhouse, and quietly but very fast, she closed the door. She leaned her forehead on the door and then looked for the phone to text Lisa.

"Are you okay?" A text came back from Lisa.

"I don't know. Please don't tell Nick. This is so embarrassing."

"Mark?"

"Yes. No. I don't know. I'll tell you when you'll get back."

"I'll ... I knew I shouldn't let him stay alone with you! I'll be there shortly."

Elli was so glad the twins woke up. She was busy to change them, to feed them. They took care of all the worries. She was so happy to be around them, to give them her entire time, her whole feelings. That's what she at least thought she was doing.

Looking at them made her see so much of Danny in them. She didn't feel loneliness. She felt in peace till now.

What on earth did I do? What has just happened? thought Elli while thinking back of herself saying those words to Mark aloud. She still felt his hands holding her face for a moment, slightly lifted toward his, so their eyes met in an uninterrupted intimacy.

"Danny, I'm so sorry! What have I done? What's wrong with me?" She felt like she can't stay with herself all of a sudden. She was so mad at herself. She did admit she missed Mark. She wished to just lay her head on him. She felt whole by him—finally like there was no need to pick herself piece by piece each day. She wasn't afraid of him—that she'll be in pain of memories the next day starting picking herself up all over again.

"Hey! Elli! Elli!" Lisa was standing for a while now beside Elli that was evidently too occupied by her own thoughts not to be able to notice her.

"Lisa, thank God you're here!"

"What did he do to you? I knew I shouldn't leave him behind."

"No. No. Lisa, wait. Slow down. It's me. I ... I ... I'm so afraid."

"What happened? Come here." Lisa gave Elli a hug. She was trembling badly. "Calm down, Elli. Please. Calm down. You know, you can't expose yourself to anything, to something that can cause your body to be like this. Shhh. Whatever happened, it's nothing that you can't handle. Remember, you're not alone."

"Lisa, I ... I ..."

"Shhh ... It's okay, Elli. Take your time," Lisa said and just held Elli quietly for a moment till she felt the trembling stopped. She took one step back. "Do you wanna sit or get a drink? How are the twins?" Lisa was trying to be strong for Elli—not to lose her patience.

"Lisa! The twins are okay. Let me just tell you what I did before I'll feel too big of a shame of it, and I'll keep it to myself." Lisa was afraid to make a sound of her taking a deep breath.

"Lisa, Mark, he, I ... Oh gosh!"

Lisa was so tempted to say something, but she just bit her lip and didn't make a sound. She felt she bit her lip to keep silent too hard. She could taste blood in her mouth, but she didn't care at this moment.

"Mark was nice. He thanked me and was about halfway downstairs when I … when I said I missed his voice! I don't know why I said that aloud! When I realized that it was too late, he … he … he was standing in front of me and holding my face in his hands."

Elli was talking very fast. Lisa didn't make a sound. She tried to even take a shallow breath to eliminate the sound. This was so romantic! But she didn't want to make a huge reaction to it. She finally felt Elli didn't shake anymore, but she looked like hell, as she did the worst mistake ever. But she felt that all of a sudden, all fell into place. Everything started to make sense—all her suspicious thoughts about Mark's presence with Elli and with the twins at the hospital, all his extra time with them. She started to smile at Elli. It was too late to hide that smile. Elli was already looking at Lisa, as she didn't understand why Lisa's reaction was a smile.

"Lisa! Why are you smiling? I did … I did a horrible thing! I'm so stupid. And it's all my fault! He won't be doing anything. But because of me and because of what I said …"

"Elli, it's okay."

"No, it's not. Danny. I shouldn't!"

"Elli, Danny will not wish anything else than you to be happy after all what you have been through! Now it all makes sense! No. I don't think so it's you. I mean I don't think you should be so hard on yourself. That you … I think, well, it's obvious after what I, I mean, we know about what Mark did, I mean how he acted the whole time. I think he'll be coming out doing this without your comment anyway. Do you understand? I saw him before. And I saw him today. He's the man, and he knows what he wants."

"Yes. Exactly! Isn't that even against some policy for the doctors? And what if he feels this way only because—"

"No, Elli! As I just said, Mark isn't someone who needs 'because.' I think, he's the one standing tall and knowing, what's the reality. Yes. He is a doctor. Goddamn attractive one. Pardon my language! But he's as well a man who I saw takes care of the twins. Sometimes seemed much more than me and Nick did! I knew … I knew it. There was something about him! About how he was falling asleep in the chair beside your bed. Reading to you. Talking to you … I knew it!"

"Lisa!" Elli was turning red. She was trying to stop Lisa in her fast and overexcited talk. But she realized it was impossible. So she just gave up. After a while, Lisa went quiet all of a sudden.

"Sorry, Elli, but I'm so happy for you! This is what you do deserve. Today, I was looking at him. At you. All of us."

"Me too."

"And?"

"And what? I have twins to take care of."

"And?"

"Lisa!"

"What?"

"Stop it! I have Danny's twins and—"

"And what? Mark seems to belong to all of you. I don't think he'll ever try to make you forget about Danny. He seems pretty much understanding how important Danny was and always will be for you and your twins. Today just felt so natural. Stop beating yourself up for it, please. Give it a chance. Please. Please."

"I don't know. It happened so fast."

"Elli, sometimes, things do happen fast in our lives. At least it seems to us, maybe because we're not thinking, preparing ourselves for it. But you can't just watch it pass by. Please, Elli. Don't let that happen! Please. Please."

"What will Nick say?"

"He likes Mark from the first meeting! He actually protected him from me so many times you can't even imagine. Believe me!"

"I'm so scared, Lisa."

"Scared of what, Elli?"

"That he'll change his mind. I'm not single. I never will be. I have twins, and that's not gonna change. And of course, I don't want that to happen."

"Elli, he knows that. He loves the twins. He loves you. Give it a chance. He's ready for you. For you and your twins. You told him those words aloud for some reason. You do have feelings for him. You might be scared by it, but I won't let you just do nothing about it. I'll not let you something so good, so real to let it pass by."

"And now what?"

"We'll get ready for a great Fourth of July. It's gonna be awesome! Tomorrow, we have a lot of things to do! Grocery shopping. You'll make the best potato salad as usual. I'll ask Nick to help me paint the swing bench tonight. So it'll have a chance to dry. And Katie will enjoy little porch lights and lots of water sprinklers! That'll be fun. I'm so excited!"

"I guess now I should tell you to calm down."

"Don't you dare. This is good being high!" They both laughed.

"I'm so nervous."

"That's great!"

"What?"

"That's great. It means you care!"

"He didn't put his helmet on."

"What?"

"When Mark was leaving from here, he didn't put his helmet on."

Lisa smiled at Elli. "He'll be okay."

Mark pulled over to the side of the road and put the helmet on. He didn't want to go home. Empty place. After such a nice evening with the twins, Elli, Lisa, Nick, and Katie, of course. He had to smile, remembering how she got him closer to all of them. He started to just drive. He enjoyed the ride, the evening city lights.

Mark couldn't wait to get through one more day to get to the Fourth of July. Thinking about it, he felt scared. "What if all those hours will get Elli space and chance to change her mind?" By thinking about that, he squeezed the bike's handles very hard and sped away from that thought.

He could still feel her skin, her hair, her breath. It was different than in the hospital—far better. It was so real before, but now, now it gave him chills just to think about it. All he wished at this moment was turn his bike around and get back as fast as he could to her and the twins. But he knew he had to keep cool and not to scare her away from him.

Mark couldn't even start picturing Lisa's reaction if she'll be seeing him back there before the fourth. At that point, he realized how late it got and how tired he was. So he automatically drove to his place, took a fast shower, and threw himself to bed. He fell asleep fast with a smile on his face.

Chapter 19

Mark woke up by the call from Sue.

"Mark?"

"Sue?"

"Hi. Good morning. Are you okay?"

"Yes. Why?"

"Well, it's 10:00 a.m. and you're not …"

"What? Ten? Oh. I'll be right there."

"Easy. No rush. I have nothing important to leave in rush for. I'm just calling because this is not your usual not to be here on time."

"I slept through. Sue, I'm sorry."

"Oh, I understand," said Sue, and her voice sounded low, disappointed.

"Oh no! Sue, it's not like you think. Really," Mark started explaining very fast. He didn't even know why. "I was just driving for a while last night after a good dinner and simply just slept through it and blew my starting time! I do apologize once more!"

"Oh. No worries. Really. It's okay. I'm glad you're okay. I think your body and mind were just exhausted for a too long time without a break."

Then Mark, all of a sudden, realized what was just happening. Instead of just apology, as he really meant he gave Sue, Dr. Raysse, his great colleague hope to believe, they'll be together. He got very upset. She was a really nice person with great heart, and he truly liked her, but ... but that was all. There was never that strong pull that was drowning him to Elli.

"I'll be right there. Is everything all right there?"

"Yes. And as I said, no rush. See you when you'll get here."

"Yes. Bye."

"Bye, Mark!"

By the time Mark had gotten to the hospital, everything turned busy, so he just shortly talked to Dr. Raysse to get situated, and she left. He felt relieved and thankful for being busy most of his working time.

He could feel her pain, but he knew she's strong, and they won't be happy together. He knew they could keep their relationship going, but it'll never be anything close to what he could see is real with Elli. He could feel love when they touched. Just the thought of her, him, them gave him chills. And he knew this is what he was longing for. He knew this is what was missing in his life.

He was worried that he'll not be enough to Elli and the twins. He would like to offer more of his time to them, but he also knew he was very dedicated to his work. Will they be okay with it?

That's what they had in common with Sue—mutual understanding. But that didn't make him run up the stairs till he could feel his heart beats crazy fast, leaving him out of breath just to think of her.

He didn't know what time he's supposed to come on the Fourth of July to Elli's place. Not too early, not too late. He wanted to just go right away after waking up, but he didn't want to look weird. After lunchtime, he was so impatient, so he decided just to get there. At that point, he didn't care how he'll look. He couldn't stand that torture.

After his arrival, all were already out in the backyard. They greeted him with smiles and open arms. The food was great as well as their chatting. The twins were adorable as usual. After putting them to sleep, Katie tricked Mark and Elli to get to the swing where they both ended up laughing while Katie and Lisa gave them first starting push. Sunset came all of a sudden. Nick finished chatting with their friendly neighbors over the fence when they all went silent by firework sounds and lights.

Mark leaned back in the swing bench with one arm stretched behind Elli's back. He looked at her profile. She was sparkling, magnetizing. He wanted to pull her closer and hold her tight. But he was afraid she needed more time. She went through so much pain and managed not to become insane. He wanted to show to her he can wait. He wanted her to know she can lay her head on him. But instead, he just pulled his hand from behind her back and took her left hand as he did so many times before. He was used to fit her hand to his own. So many times, but she, did she know about it when that was back then? In the hospital? Many times he fell asleep while holding her little hand in his. But did she know that? Could she feel that? Could she remember anything from the time when lying in the hospital bed, with all those machines monitoring all her functions? He wished she could remember him. He wished she could remember something from their time together.

She held her breath for a second but didn't pull her hand away. Mark wasn't holding her too tight, even when he wanted to, to not get her chance to pull her hand away. But he chose to give her the space to make her own decision.

He got so happy. But he held back not to scream loud of happiness.

Katie commented good or not so great; well, now she called it terrible-horrible pieces of firework. By the final, she hopped on the swing bench between them, so they moved the swing more up to the air.

Mark and Elli shared short look over Katie's head, both of them like they never have been afraid of pain.

After the fireworks, Mark was going to help them clear the stuff from the backyard, but Lisa stopped him. She said something about his long busy day at work, while they're all off. Elli smiled by that and commented, that not exactly all since the twins were really demanding more attention. All off them laughed.

Elli walked Mark to the door. She went very quiet, but her eyes were smiling happily. She felt safe and happy in her small bubble world. Mark took his time to look at her, to take with him her smile, her moves. Before he said anything, he had to clear up his throat. And even the rest of them were still busy with the cleanup outside, he said, "Elli, thank you for this amazing afternoon. May I call you tomorrow after work?"

"Yes," said Elli, and now it was her who needed to clear the throat. "Yes, it'll be nice to hear your voice." "Good night, Elli. I'll talk to you tomorrow." "Good night," Elli said and smiled at Mark.

He was turning toward the stairs, but he couldn't walk away from her just like that. He turned back quickly, face to face with her. He caught fear in her eyes. He pulled her closer to him and felt her body leaning at his. Tense was melting away. He knew he'll try to make it all better piece by piece.

"I'll wait, Elli. I promised you never have to be afraid. Good night, Elli." He gave her a short kiss that she couldn't even react to and released her gently with one more fast look and smiled at her before he ran down the stairs to his motorcycle. And as the last time, he just sat happily on it and drove away.

And he did it again. No helmet! thought Elli. Just wait till tomorrow, Mark!

Their talk over the phone was very warm, happy, and easy till Elli made a pause. Mark sort of panicked. He couldn't see her. He needed to see her face to know all is okay when all of a sudden, Elli broke the silence. "Mark, did you really mean it? You promise I don't have to be ever afraid?" She could feel his sight of relief.

"Yes, Elli. Everything I ever told you, I mean it."

"So how come you're speeding away on your speed bike without the helmet on?"

She felt as though his laugh was relaxed on the other side.

"You noticed that? I was hoping you didn't."

"Of course, I did. I even said please drive carefully, but you couldn't hear that."

"No. I didn't hear that. But, Elli, I want you to know that I do always wear a helmet, and both of the times I did realize that while driving away from you, and I did stop and put it on, and it was each time, gosh, Elli … I had, honestly, I had full head of you."

They both went quiet. Elli closed her eyes while she felt chills get through her whole body. She felt weak. But good. So confusing.

Mark, on the other side, bit his lip. He was scared he said too soon too much. But shouldn't you be open no matter what with the person you feel so much to? For a moment, he couldn't even hear her breath, but the call wasn't disconnected. He took that as a good sign. Then he did hear her breath. But none of them was able to speak.

"I know, Elli. I'm sometimes impulsive, but I do always tell what's on my mind. I'll never hide any feelings or thoughts away from you. I'm so happy and in balance by you. By you, the twins, Katie, Lisa, yes, I know, I know, even by Lisa that seems to be enjoying giving me the hard time, and Nick. I feel each time as I do belong to all of you. Elli, please say something. If the helmet

... Okay, if me not putting the helmet on makes you worried, I think you too do feel something ... special." That's when his voice got in trouble "Between us."

Elli cleared her throat quietly and tried to ease up the conversation. She tried to be rational, calm, and playful. "So you're saying no more riding on the bike without helmet?"

"God, women! That's all you'll say now?"

"I didn't hear the answer. Did I miss it?"

"Elli, no more riding the bike without helmet. You have my word!"

"Hmm ... and how are you going to do that, to keep your word when you'll be leaving our place again?" said Elli and smiled.

"Believe me, it'll be hard, but I'll better put the helmet on before I'll even touch the bike. Otherwise, you have my permission grounded me from bike riding, but please, don't be too hard since the only reason will be you."

"Then for me, be safe, don't get hurt, or ... please, Mark."

He didn't want her to be hurt again. He saw before tears rolling down her fair skin, and it was so hard to see her breaking down and not be able to do more than he did. Nobody was around them, at least that's what he thought. He didn't know Dr. Sue was watching him from the other room, seeing him take washcloth and gently wipe away tears from both sides and leaning closer to her while talking to her quietly. Elli's face looked immediately relaxed, like he did comfort her. That's why she didn't interrupt. She knew she had to put the patient's needs in front of the personal ones, even if they were her own. It was very painful to see how much someone who she love was having those great feelings for someone else. But there was a hope once Elli will be gone from the hospital, will be also gone from Mark's and her life. They were such a great team before she happened to be between them. She decided to wait. Things will get one day back to normal.

She saw Mark straightening his torso and slowly moved her hair away from her face. Then take the book and started to read aloud. Then she quietly stepped out of the sight.

"I will, Elli. I gave you my promise. I don't want you to be ever afraid. And I'm planning to keep my promise. That's who I am. I do keep my promises. You can ask!" Mark said and smiled.

She could feel he was smiling. She was too. She was ... just a human who he built up after she felt apart— together with Lisa and Nick.

"I ... I won't ask, Mark. I do believe you. And I'm glad it's me who's your head full of!"

"Elli, I have to go. Case. I'm still at work. Can I, can I see you tonight or tomorrow?"

"I would like to see you tonight, but if you'll be too tired, I'll understand."

"Not so much as you from the twins! So I'll see you tonight. I can't wait!"

"Helmet!"

"What?"

"Don't forget to wear a helmet!"

He chuckled. "How could I? See you tonight, Elli! I can't wait to see you, to hold you! The twins as well, of course." His voice disappeared, and she could hear for a second the familiar hospital sound before the phone call ended. The room was so quiet, as everything had stopped for a moment. She missed him already—his voice, his words, his chuckling. She was still holding the phone close to her ear, and she started smiling by remembering Mark's chuckling. She didn't even notice Nick was standing for a while in the hallway, looking at her and smiling as well. He cleared out his throat so she can notice him.

"Nick!"

"Hi, Elli. I just thought I'll drop off some potatoes when I saw you standing here. You were smiling! Mark?"

"What?"

"You are still holding the phone by your ear," Nick said and smiled.

"I assume you're calling to Mark."

Elli's face blushed. She just quietly answered, "Yes. But—"

"But what?"

"Nick, I feel sort of guilty toward the twins and ... and Danny."

"Elli, Danny, I know I didn't know him personally, but from what I know, this is exactly what he was wishing it's gonna happen. Mark seems to be a good man. I do believe from the moment that I saw him by you or by the twins through the time while you all were in the hospital—that he really cares about you all, and even after spending some time here, he does have feelings for you."

"What if he is just sort of attached to us as patients? You know what I mean. He even might get into trouble for it, can't he?"

"He can handle it, if yes. But I think you can cross out that doctor-patient attachment relationship from your thoughts. I think it's obvious by the way he looks at you, his whole-body language toward you ..." Elli blushed again.

"And it's okay to keep memories of Danny. I think Mark will be cool with it if you talk to him about it. Just please not all the time, okay? That will be too hard for any person even the one most in love, most understanding. Danny will be honored each day by all of us, and the twins will know about him. But life must keep moving forward no matter how much it hurts. And I personally think you're doing great! So no guilty feelings, please, Elli. Okay?"

"Okay. Thank you, Nick."

The day went busy for Elli at home just as well for Mark at the hospital. He couldn't wait to be done at work so he can run those few stairs up and ring the bell. He'll just knock on the door just in case the twins will be asleep.

Elli was frequently looking at the clock. If it will be in her power, she'll be turning the time forward to have Mark there. Just thinking of him got her smile on her face. After the twins went for a nap, she went to the kitchen and cooked light dinner. She texted earlier to Lisa that she'll have dinner for her and Nick.

When they were halfway through the dinner, the twins were fully awake entertaining them, there was knocking on the door.

Elli smiled and ran to the door. She opened them too fast and accidentally hit Mark that was evidently standing too close to them.

"Oh, I'm so sorry! Are you okay?"

"I'm okay," said Mark as he backed up and automatically held the spot on his head where he got hit. "I think I should keep the helmet on till I'll be let in." They both laughed.

"I'm really sorry, Mark."

They looked at each other with smiles on their faces. "Come on in," yelled Lisa from the kitchen.

"Full household?"

"Yes. Sorry."

"What are you sorry for? That's great! Hello, everyone. It's so good to see you all."

"Hi, Mark. How are you?"

"I'm good. A little tired. It was a pretty busy day at work, but I'm okay."

"Tell me something about that," said Lisa while giving a look to Elli.

"We missed Elli there. They didn't hire anybody after she left, but they split her work between all of us."

"Poor you," said Elli while watching Mark already holding one of the twins in his arms. And he looked at Lisa.

"You're not trying to get Elli back to work? Lisa?" "Well, we love her meals after we're coming back home," Lisa said and laughed. "But I do miss her there. My lunch body. You know how boring it is to be there without her?"

"I guess it doesn't count much that I took you today for lunch."

"Of course, it does, Nick."

Mark was already looking at Elli. She knew what he wanted to ask, so she asked him first if he's hungry and did offer what was cooked. Mark did all of a sudden felt his hunger since he stopped just for a short time at home to get shower and changed the clothes. But more than that, he wanted to know what Elli was planning to do. He didn't think it was okay for her to go back to work. He thought it was still too soon.

"Elli, what are you thinking about going back to work?"

"So are you hungry?"

"You didn't answer to me."

"You didn't answer to me."

They both were looking at each other.

"I do miss work. I love the twins, but day passed day, and I feel like I don't even know if it's Monday or Sunday. Everything blends. I was asked to go back, but I didn't say yes or no. I asked for some time to make the right decision."

"What about the twins?" asked Mark, but before Elli could answer, he already asked another question. "What about Sue? Have you talked to her?" Mark felt like his mind was about to explode. "And yes, I'm hungry. I went home straight from work, but I only took time to take a fast shower before coming here." Now his face was turning a little bit more red.

Nick and Lisa exchanged fast looks and smiles, but they kept quiet, just purely enjoying the conversation and all reactions between Elli and Mark. They seemed like they were the only one in the moment in the room. Elli didn't even ask him what he would like to eat or how much to put it on the plate. She just naturally took the plate and filled it up. When she handed the plate to Mark, she realized she didn't ask.

"Oh, sorry, Mark. Is this okay?"

"Yes. Thank you."

"You're welcome, and no, I didn't talk to Dr. Raysse yet."

"But you will, right? Before you'll make your final decision."

"Yes, I already left her a message that I would like to talk to her."

"Good," said Mark with relief in his voice. He did understand all what Elli felt, but he was crazy scared it will be overwhelming for her. He could just imagine how getting to work and all around the twins will be for her. For them.

"All right, Elli, thank you very much for a great meal. We'll put the twins to the cribs, and we will go. I have some projects that I still need to work on tonight."

"What? We were talking about trying our best not to bring any work home."

"I did. But if you insist, I'll take it now back to the work," said Nick in a teasing voice.

"No! You!"

"Okay. Let's get these a little clean up and to the bed." "I'll do it," said Elli.

"You can do it tomorrow," said Lisa with a wink toward Mark.

"Plus, Mark, I'm sure will enjoy you more here."

"Thank you, guys." Elli's voice was failing her a little, so she just turned away to take the plate for herself and peacefully joined Mark in eating her dinner. They did that many times in the hospital, so they didn't even think how it looked to Lisa and Nick that they exchanged each other's look with quite understanding, and Nick pulled Lisa faster away with the twins in arms before she'll be able to say something aloud. He was sure she was about to. His Lisa!

"Thank you, Elli. It was delicious."

"You're welcome. Were you having enough?"

"I sure did! I'm so stuffed. Would you like to go for a walk?"

"The twins. But sure."

"Sorry. We can just take monitor and go on the backyard."

"We can, but I'll ask Lisa and Nick if they will stick here for ten to fifteen minutes more so we can even go for a short walk. I would love that as well."

Shortly, both of them ran down the stairs and walked toward the sunset.

"Isn't it beautiful?"

"Not as much as you, Elli," said Mark while looking at Elli's profile.

Elli just silently looked at Mark and smiled. She was happy. She didn't even realize how, but Mark was already holding her hand in his. Her hand felt colder, but to Mark, it felt great since his was usually warm.

"Your hand feel so nice ... cooling me."

"Yours is warming mine very nice. Mark?"

"Yes?"

"I was thinking ..."

"Elli, can we talk about that after walk when we will get back?" He was afraid he's not able to think straight. He felt chills. He was happy just to hold her hand and walk quietly by her side. He couldn't ask for more. Could he? He didn't want to ruin this moment. Something was telling him; something bothered her, and he wasn't focused at all.

"Sure," Elli said, and Mark felt she did relax herself a little bit. He felt her love and trust in him, and he wasn't planning to lose it. So they just kept going in silent till he pointed out it's time to turn back to switch Lisa and Nick.

Elli thanked Lisa and Nick, and with the monitor, she stepped out on the backyard toward Mark who waived to them, saying good night. Mark went straight to the swing bench and left the place for Elli to sit beside him, which she did, but she left a quiet space between them. He noticed that right away, but he was patient. He just started to swing the bench a little bit.

"Elli?"

"Yes?"

"Just say it. There was something evidently important for you, what you were about to tell me on the walk, and I see you're tense now. I did only ask you to wait to tell me about it later, because I couldn't focus. Now I'm all yours."

"Okay. I want you to know I do enjoy every time we are together. But ..."

"There's no but, Elli. I do feel the same," Mark said while he pulled her closer to him.

"Please, don't interrupt me. I'm losing my focus on what I need to tell you."

Nick had to pull Lisa twice away from the window. She was sensing Elli may do some mistake. She was worried. She was glad to see her happy, bright up while talking about Mark, while being by him.

The second time Nick pulled her away from the window, he told her about their conversation about what had worried Elli.

"Nick, why on earth didn't you tell me about that?"

"Hmm, I think you can remember well what we did that day."

"Okay, okay. But what if she will make a crazy mistake now?"

"I trust her, Lisa. I believe she can handle it."

"Look at her! Maybe we should get out there before it'll be too late."

"Trust her more. And I think Mark isn't an unsteady person. I think he'll handle it."

"He might be that all, but Elli is stubborn as—"

"Let's wait. Give them space and time, please," Nick said and gave her a kiss.

Mark went silent, but he turned more toward Elli to see all her emotions on her face.

"I love to be by your side, but I think you're such a great person who deserves to be with someone who you'll love, with someone who doesn't have so much on the plate … someone with whom it'll all be more simple. I'm … I'm a mom in the first place, and nothing's going to change that. And I'll have probably always by my side Lisa, Nick and Katie as well," Elli said to ease up the talk. "I don't think it's fair to you. You could pick anyone. Have your own kid. Or kids. Plus I'm afraid you'll have trouble at work because of me, us. You know what I mean. And I … I just don't have the whole time of the world. And I even didn't get back to work—which I will. There are money, crazy money from … from Danny." She paused from her talk to make sure the tears that appeared in her eyes stay in. "But I … I can't … I don't want to touch them. Kids can use them one day, but we won't need them. I can manage to provide for all they need. And I think Dr. Raysse likes you more than a colleague." After this long monologue, Elli went silent. Just then, she looked up at Mark. He was looking straight into Elli's eyes with so much love and pain at the same time but remained quiet. He gently pulled her hair away from her face. She closed her eyes, keeping the moment for her memories when he'll walk away from her, from them. She knew at this point she felt a lot to Mark, but she reminded herself to be real, to keep her feet on the ground, and to be fair. She made peace with herself that it'll be easier to let him go now than when she and the kids will get more attached.

Mark wasn't evidently going to break the silence. So Elli caught her breath and said, "It's okay, Mark. I understand. And it'll be probably better. I mean that's probably the best decision. Of course, I'll be glad if we'll stay ... in touch ... I mean ... you know what I mean ... as friends. Nick and Lisa adore you as well."

Mark just kept looking into her eyes, without any words. But he let the bench stop on its own.

"Do you want me to walk you out?" asked Elli quietly. She felt a sharp pain of sadness, knowing she's going to walk away the man who is having such a deep meaning and value in her eyes. She was about to stand up, when...

At that time, Lisa dragged Nick to the window. She was getting so nervous. It took lots of effort from Nick to keep her from running straight between them.

"Lisa, whatever it is, it's about to change both of their lives."

"Exactly. That's what I'm trying to tell you the entire time! And we both can tell this isn't going well. And we both can tell they do fit so well together. If we can see that, how should we be just letting them do stupid thing?"

"Because they need to stay together because they both want to and not because someone will tell them to do so. And we can't be around them all the time to keep them together, with the help of other's point of view."

"But, Nick, we are here. We are here right now, and if we are the only one who can see clearly and who can help, then we should!"

"Come here, sweetheart, calm down and watch. I do believe Mark will handle it. Whatever it is." Nick hugged Lisa for comfort and stayed still with her by the window.

Mark pulled Elli down all the way on his lap. She lost the balance just a little bit but enough to put her hands on his chest to catch it back. Her face blushed when she realized she felt his chest, his heartbeat. Their hearts were both beating like in a race. Her body felt a nicely warm wave that gave her chills and made her close her eyes to fully enjoy it. When she realized it, Mark kissed her shortly like before. But when she opened her eyes and tried to do any other reaction, he kissed her again; but this time, it wasn't just a fast kiss. It was warm and passionate. Her head felt spinning, so all she could do was close her eyes and hold him tight as much as possible with both of her hands behind his neck at this time. One of her hands went from his neck skin and into the hair, and then she realized she was kissing him back. She sighed with pleasure, and then she freaked out and tried to say his name, but she felt she was losing it.

"Elli, I wanna be with you, with the twins, with Lisa, Nick, Katie, and whoever belongs to you. I respect Danny's memory, and I'll make sure the twins will know him as you remembered him. I'm just worried if I'm gonna be good enough to deserve all of you since yes, I'm a doctor. This is my life, and this is who I am. That's why I understand why you would like to go to work." "Well, mine isn't nothing like yours …"

"But it has a meaning to you too. To Sue. Dr. Raysse. Yes. We do understand each other. We are a good team at work. And honestly, we … there was a time when we were together, and I know she still have feelings for me. She is a great person, and I wish her well, but I've realized something is missing. And I'm not able to put it to words, and maybe, I hope I ever won't be, but I feel … you make me feel like this like no other women ever did. It's … it's different. So many reasons which I can start telling you what makes me keep coming back to you … to you all …"

"But it's a short time …"

"Not really, sweetheart. It's been months. To me, every minute counts from the moment I saw you."

"That's not fair. I had no clue what was happening back then!"

"I can start telling you all, but you did remember my voice! I know you did it! And it's nothing about patient- doctor relation, and if, for any reason, the hospital will try to get me a hard time about it, please, let me face it. Let me take care of it.

I love the twins as my own. And who knows one day if you, if we will feel we would like to have our one or how many you, we will wish to have, we'll talk about that then."

Elli realized she got lost again in his kissing. It made her automatically close her eyes when she felt Mark stood up with her still in his arms. He only stopped kissing her for a time to whisper to her ears how much he would love to make love to her and then continue to kissing her while walking toward the house.

Elli broke the kiss with only one word coming out of her mouth: "Monitor."

They both started to laugh insanely happy. Mark backed up and grabbed the monitor while holding Elli still in his arms. She was still not with her weight back, so he did manage that without any problem.

At that moment, Nick kissed Lisa on the back side of her neck and whispered into her ears, "I think we've got the best ending of their conversation, and we should try our best ending of the day as well. What do you think?"

Lisa turned face to face with Nick, with teasing question about his work project when he kissed her and threw her gently on the bed with his body following instantly after. Their silliness was filling up the air.

Meanwhile, Mark carried Elli upstairs to the house and quietly closed the door behind them.

"Elli, I'm so madly in love with you. I love you more every day, and all I could think of is to wish I can be everything you need. I feel you all are mine, a deeper meaning for life that I was longing for. I know what I feel. Please, don't try to push me away from you again… I made many mistakes in my life, and I'm sure I'll do many more, but losing you will be the biggest one."

She was standing silly on his feet holding him tight with her hands wrapped behind his back. He was holding her face in his hands and leaning over her. The pain in her eyes was gone. They both leaned their foreheads on each other and smiled while looking into each other's eyes.

At the same time, they slowly started to remove their clothes piece by piece. Mark followed her spine line, from the beginning all the way down. Elli's body shook with pleasure and chill. She let both of her hands slide down by the sides of his body. Mark closed his eyes and let it out dreamingly. "Elli." He lifted her up on his waist and sat down on the edge of the bed, kissing her. Leaning her to the back with her legs wrapped around his waist.

"Elli, I never ever wanted to make anybody happy any possible way, how I would like to make you happy since day one, and I'll try my best to do so every day."

"Mark." Elli was looking at him, and tears were rolling down her cheeks, her breasts, ending on her legs. Mark started to slowly kiss every single drop that he could reach, where one he couldn't, he gently wiped off by the other side of his hands while he turned Elli, keeping her close to his body and lay her on her back, leaning with his body weight but trying to lift up some of it to not hurt her since she was still getting stronger every day— recovering. But she pulled him gently all the way down on her. She felt his excitement escalate, and his hand felt how excited she was.

"Elli."

"What?" Elli teased him with the question while she pulled a little bit away to catch her breath.

"How can I be so lucky?" Then he closed his eyes when he felt her gentle touch going down his torso all the way down between his legs. He kissed her slowly all the way down while his hand lifted her lower part of the body, and she felt all the muscle work while he kept going with his tongue on her sensitive parts. He left one hand for support under her while she lifted her legs. After she felt weak, she reached out for a pillow, but it was too far, so Mark reached out for it and handed it to her. Then he put his hand behind her neck and lifted her head to kiss her again till she grabbed his bottom passionately, and he sighed to her ear, "Elli, I can't wait any longer, may I?"

She didn't answer in the words, but he felt her hand navigating his own. He turned her on top of his body when their bodies become one. She straightened up her torso, and he felt how she shook by the chill. He pulled her forward and back and once more, over and over till she leaned closer to him to give him a kiss and then caress his ear, his breasts, and his nipples. That's when he couldn't take it anymore, and he turned her under him. They were both breathing heavily. Their bodies heated up. Every touch did count. He was as close to her as he ever could be. She let out a lowered scream with voice fueled by pleasure. A little bit after enjoying looking at her, Mark started to make moves slowly in and out. Her hands touched his torso once again, and they smiled gently at each other. Then they both enjoyed their closeness and movements that felt so nice. Mark sped up till he lay down his body happily beside Elli. He pulled her closer. She snuggled under his arm. He felt her trembling, so he pulled the cover to warm her up.

"Elli, do you want me to bring you a drink?"

"No, I'm fine. Thank you, Mark. What about you?"

"Not now. I'll get it later."

She fell asleep while he stepped to the bathroom for a moment. He went for a glass of water and checked on the twins that were both peacefully asleep. He set the alarm clock and slid his body beside Elli's under the cover. She turned in her sleep to him. Moonlight touched her face. She was smiling. He felt so happy but managed himself to not squeeze her tight. He knew he should even force her to have at least few sips of water. But he didn't, so at least he needed to let her recharge energy in sleep. He put a glass with water on her side, easy to reach when she'll wake up.

Chapter 20

It felt like he slept only for a few minutes when, as a robot, he tapped off the alarm and got up and out of the bed quietly as much as possible. He dressed up in the bathroom when Elli appeared, still naked in the doorway. But she stood on the side of the door frame and the wall, covering herself as much as possible.

She said quietly, "Hi."

"Hi, Elli. The twins are okay. I just did check up on them. I brought a glass of water for you. I'm sorry if I woke you up."

"Thank you, Mark," said Elli while Mark took her bathrobe off the hook and wrapped her gently like a most precious gift.

"Oh, Elli. I'm so sorry I have to leave."

"Mark, it's okay. We both know. You don't need to be physically by me, us 24/7."

"But I want to."

"And you also need to, and you do want to be working. And you are very needed there." While saying so, Elli gave him hug, and he lifted her up again into his arms.

"Oh. You shouldn't do that," Elli said, but she felt dizzy and was happy he did it. Mark put her nicely to bed and helped her put the pajama on and covered her with duvet cover as she liked all the way up under her chin. He did remember.

"Mark, thank you for—"

"Elli, pssst. You don't need to thank me for that."

"I'm sorry I won't walk with you downstairs."

"Don't be silly. I'm very sorry I made you stay up so late and waste so much of your energy."

"There was no wasting. It was all well used."

"But I should know better. My dear Elli. I'll lock the door so you don't have to worry about that. I miss you already." They kissed passionately, but she interrupted and gave him a weak smile.

"I don't want to be the reason for you to be late." When she said so, she drifted away to her dreams. All that Mark wished at that moment was to just take his clothes off and slide beside Elli. But he knew she was right. So instead of that, he stepped quietly out to the early morning fresh air. He didn't even stop at his place. He went straight to the hospital. He set the alarm for one hour earlier so he can get earlier to the hospital and, if lucky, stretch the sleep for two to three more hours. He dressed up quickly and fell asleep, probably at the moment his head touched one of the hospital pillows.

He woke up by Sue's voice. "Rough night?"

"Not at all," said Mark very shortly. "How is everything here?"

"I think you can stretch your sleep for another two hours."

"Thanks, Sue. That's exactly what I was looking for."

"Sure. I'll tell the nurse she can find you here," said Sue while walking out of the room and heading out of the hospital. She sat into her car but didn't start it. Instead of starting the car, she started to cry. She finally admitted to herself anything between her and Mark is gone for good. She knew it'll be tough to get over it, but she knew one day she will. She was hurt. She was mad. She only assumed it was Elli. But she knew her for a while; she knew her life story, and she didn't have the heart or the strength to be mad at her. Plus Elli didn't know about them, about their "understandable" relationship. And if it is someone new, someone different, well, it doesn't matter; it's not her. He is seeing someone else, and that's the bottom line. She wasn't crying anymore, but she just rested her body on the seat with her eyes closed. They were burning so badly. That's why she decided not to start the car and just rest for a while. She felt too down to do a thing. All of a sudden, she thought she heard a knocking. But she just didn't want to pay any attention to it. She's in the car. Who'll be knocking on the car? But the sound did repeat once more. She forced herself to turn her head toward the window with her eyelids still closed.

"Sue!"

By hearing her own name called, she realized that the knocking that she so successfully ignored in the beginning was real, and it was Mark who was waiting for her to turn her head.

"Sue?"

"Mark, hi."

"What are you doing here? Are you alright?"

"Yes! Everything is just 'fine'!"

"Did you just cry, Sue?"

"Me? Yes. I did. But it's okay now. I just rested for a while, and I'm okay to go. But what about you? What are you doing outside? Shouldn't you be inside?"

"Are you sure you're okay? You look horrible."

"Thanks, Mark. That's exactly what I needed to hear right now!" said Sue with little sarcastic grin.

"Come on, Sue. You know I didn't mean to hurt your feelings or self-esteem," said Mark, and they both smiled.

"Why are you here? You didn't answer to me."

"I saw your car still on parking lot, so I just came out to see if everything is okay."

"It will be, Mark. Someday it'll be."

"Oh. I'm sorry, Sue. You're an amazing person, and I wish I felt something just like—"

Sue didn't let him finished. She knew he didn't try to hurt her on purpose. But she was hurt. She was tired. She was upset—with only one thing on her mind. "Who?" she said quietly.

"What?" asked Mark, who couldn't hear a thing since Sue did ask quietly, and the nearest car did noise while leaving the hospital parking.

"Who is she?"

"Sue. Really? Is that gonna make any difference?"

"For me, yes. Just say it. If it's just some girl, I'll ... we'll still have a chance, but if it is ..." Sue went quiet all of a sudden.

"If it is?"

"Mark, please, just say it. Please!" At that moment, she was looking at Mark.

"Are you sure, Sue?"

"Yes, I am. I think I know the answer now, but I need to hear it from you."

"Elli. It's Elli."

At the moment, when Mark let out Elli's name, she started crying again. She couldn't stop.

"I'm sorry for my cry. I'm happy for you—for both of you. I do wish I was the one. I do wish because you're a great man, Mark. But I knew something was missing, and for some reason, I had the feeling when I saw you with her, you found what you were looking for."

"Come here, Sue." Mark leaned through the open window and gave her a hug. "I'll be always here for you. I promise."

"You don't have to promise me that, Mark. I know you will. Thank you. Hope you guys will make it through all."

"Thank you. And I'm sure there is someone somewhere just for you."

"Let's hope for it."

"Are you sure you'll be okay to drive? I can call you a taxi."

"I'm good," said Sue with a sad smile on her face.

"All right then. Please let me know you did arrive home, okay?"

"Okay. I will. Bye, Mark."

"Bye, Sue. I'll be waiting for your call or at least your text. Don't forget about that!"

"I won't."

After that, Sue started the car and left. Mark was standing at the same spot till she disappeared from his view. He was upset, but he knew there was nothing else he could do for her at this moment. His face lit up once he started thinking of Elli. Everything felt so good. But even he felt her understanding of who he is, his lifestyle, Mark was still questioning—if he won't disappoint her, them. He slowly turned and started walking toward the hospital when he felt his phone vibrating. It was a simple text from Elli, just a picture of the heart. Mark smiled and was about to reply when the nurse called to him and hurried him to return to the hospital.

Elli was waiting for Mark's reply, but nothing was coming. She was busy with the twins but unusually impatient. She'll end up calling Lisa. Her first reaction was about if anything did happen. They were already talking over the phone two hours in the morning. So she didn't have to act like she doesn't know how things went last evening.

"Yes! He didn't text back!"

"Are you serious? Elli, you are the most patient person in the world, and now you're stressing out over a text?"

"Text from Mark. That's the difference."

"Not enough for excuse," Lisa said and started to giggle.

"Hey. That's being rude."

"Is it? Sorry. You know, Elli, it wasn't meant like this."

"Wasn't? You're obviously teasing me!"

"Okay. I'll stop. Right at this moment. Okay?"

"Thanks."

"And now listen," said Lisa while clearing her throat. Elli went completely silent on the other side. "You have just recently been in the hospital."

"Yes! So?"

"So you got a perfect picture of how things are functioning there. I'm 100 percent sure this is what happened. And I can put a bid on it! You did text Mark, and he got your text. His face did light up like Christmas tree. Even I have no idea what was in it. He did read it, and in the moment he was about to text you back, they call him to the patient."

"And that's why I called you to hear!"

"Elli, come on! What else do you want me to tell you? What do you want to hear?"

"I don't know, Lisa. Maybe just something … something else

… different than this. This just sounds as …" "As a cliché?"

"Yes. See, even you can see it this way."

"Yes. But, Elli, isn't this the most possible thing that might really happen?"

"Yes. It might."

"So by the way, what was in the text?"

"Lisa!"

"What? It's not as I called you to talk about the text. So now after the whole discussion, I do feel I would like to know. And I think I do deserve to know."

"Do you?"

"Yes. Definitely. Now I'm sure. Come on, Elli, don't let me keep waiting."

"A heart," said Elli. Lisa was still quiet. She didn't want to interrupt Elli, but she couldn't hear anything else coming from Elli.

"A heart?"

"Yes. A heart."

"Nothing else?"

"Nothing else."

"A heart. That's ... that's an original. A heart. A picture of it. Okay. I was expecting something ..."

"Something more? Like whole story written in a short text?" Elli said and giggled.

"Okay. Okay. You don't have to be laughing at me."

"I should probably ask you what you did write in your last text to Nick."

"Ha! Funny! Really funny. No. I don't think you want to know what's in my last text to Nick."

"Okay. I trust your decision. Keep it. Don't share it with me. Sometimes it is really less more. And I think this is exactly that moment."

"Oh. You have no idea, Elli, how I got relieved by that!"

"I can almost see it, even when you are somewhere there on the other side of the line."

"Yes. And that other side is work. Like a real work."

"Thanks. Now it will feel just great to continue to just take care of the twins."

"You know what I meant."

"Yes, I know. And believe me, if I could find any words to describe what I felt, I would rather send that than that ... heart picture. But I just couldn't. I just felt that great feeling, and I wanted to reach out to him."

"You're something, Elli. But that's I think exactly what Mark is enjoying so much with you. You're our original."

"What if he'll change his mind? It's so much, maybe too much for him. Work. Me. The twins. Sue."

"What about her?"

"They're together before us. They do have the same lifestyle. Thinking. They know how to support each other. Comfort. But me?"

"You are exactly what he needed. What he was longing for ... to get his life balanced. Not work at work and work in his personal life. Which, speaking of work, I should do something productive till I'm at work. But, Elli, Mark did choose you. He is the man with great priorities and great heart. He's honest. I'm sure he'll tell honestly to Sue how everything is. I can see on him how much he does care about you and the twins as well. I saw it long time ago. I just, I was just very protective of you, so I misread his look at you. Today, I know. Now I understand. It was the look of gentle and caring love—in the way he did look at you and in everything else he did around you. Gosh. I hope he won't want me to be apologizing for the rest of our lives for it."

"I think he will," Elli said and finally laughed the whole situation. "One day, when we all will grow old, we will be sitting all together, and then Mark will most likely turned toward you with words: 'Lisa, do you remember?' And you'll interrupt him because, of course, you'll be impatient to finally hear what's on his mind. Then he'll repeat just to make you wait a little bit longer to what he has to say, and he will finish describing how you did accuse him, being suspicious instead of seeing his pure, true feelings to me and the twins."

"Unfortunately, this is most likely to happen few years from now. Let's just hope Nick will be right there, not joining Mark but trying his best to ease up the situation."

"I'm sure he will. And if for some reason he won't, I'll step in. Don't you worry."

"Elli."

"Yes?"

"I'm so happy you're back. You know what I mean. I missed you so much. Okay. I'm going to do some work, but you, when kids will fall asleep, please forget about to-do list. Take a rest! Please!"

"Okay, I will. The truth is, I do feel exhausted. Already."

"Don't push yourself till you'll get too weak. Please. And stop thinking about Mark. Put the smile on your lips. He is yours. Completely. And you know it. You can feel it. Text me if anything. Okay?"

"I will. Thanks, Lisa!"

They ended conversation, and Elli did put smile on her face. She thought of Mark. She thought of Danny. She checked on the twins and fell asleep in the chair in their room. She was very tired and sleepy she forgot to eat through the whole day.

She woke up by Mark and Lisa's voices. She thought at first she was just dreaming about them. But once she opened her eyes, she saw Mark's very pale face.

"Elli, are you okay? You scared me so much, girl!"

"Mark. Hi! Ouch!"

"What. What hurts?"

"Nothing. I'm okay."

"You don't say ouch when you're okay."

"What are you two doing here? Did it already get so late?"

"No. I have break, and Lisa just came because you're not responding to her texts."

"I'm sorry, Lisa. After our talk, I must really just put that smile on my face and then fall asleep happily. Will you guys eat something small before you'll need to head back?"

"Elli, Elli, I think you're the one who needs to eat and drink something. Lisa, help me. Please. When was the last time you eat or drink something?"

"It was the water from you, Mark. I just got busy after with the cooking and the twins."

"And, Lisa, I've got it."

"Hey, it's not my fault she didn't eat or drink."

"I know. I'm sorry, Lisa. It's not even her fault. She's not like me. I'll eat half before the cooking is done." With this true comment, Mark did ease up the situation. They helped Elli get to the kitchen when one of the twins woke up.

"I'll go," said Lisa. "Thank you, Lisa."

"Thanks. I'll get Elli something to boost her blood sugar fast."

"You just did, Mark," said Elli quietly.

"I did what?" Mark said while he kept looking around for food to help Elli faster.

"You're here. That's the biggest, sweetest blood sugar boost up ever, isn't it?"

"Elli," said Mark, and in that moment, his eyes looked at Elli with the softest look the eyes can do. He kneeled down and gave her a kiss.

"Hmm … Hmm …" Lisa cleared out her throat while stepping into the situation. "Did you get her something to eat or drink? Oh boy. Glad I came as well."

By these words, all of them giggled, and Elli's face was regaining colors.

"Please, Elli, don't you ever do that again. I don't want to even think what could happen if we won't come."

"I'm truly sorry."

"She is. Believe her. She was just too occupied by the thought you didn't respond to her text."

"Thanks, Lisa," said Elli, with blush coming to her cheeks.

"I was going to. That text, it made me smile, but when I was going to text you back …" At that moment, Lisa was quietly finishing the explanation word by word with Mark that made him turn to her.

"Sorry, but that is exactly what I told her. Didn't I, Elli?"

"Yes, you did."

"You have been busy girls as I see," Mark said and winked at Elli with a smile.

"Oh gosh. Now this is embarrassing."

"It's not, Elli. That's what I like about you. My Elli. All right. My time's up. Lisa, are you going to be okay to get back to work? I can give you a ride."

"Yeah. I'll be fine." All of a sudden, Lisa started to cry. "I'm so sorry. I just got so scared. It was like … I'm sorry."

"Lisa, it's okay!" Mark gave Lisa the same hot chocolate in the big mug as she did to Elli. "Drink it. Both of you."

"Thank you, Mark. Go. Don't worry. We will be okay," said Elli.

"I know. I'll see you after work. Be good, girl."

"I will. We will."

The house went quiet once the twins finished their bath and dinner and were tucked into their beds. Mark ate a late dinner with Elli as they talked about their days. After they were done with their meals, he put the dishes to the sink and lifted up Elli just like the other day.

"Mark, you can put me down," said Elli while laughing to his skin on the neck while trying to keep the balance by wrapping her hands around his neck. "I'm okay to walk."

"I know you are. But you deserved this yesterday, today, and tomorrow as well."

"You're tired. I don't want you to get hurt."

"Then hold tight so we won't fall. Dishes can wait till tomorrow."

They smiled at each other. Both very exhausted but happy. Mark placed Elli gently on the bed. He saw she was trying to hide away from him the pain from neck toward the left shoulder. He asked her to sit at the edge of the bed. She looked at him with questions in her eyes, but there was no need to answer. So she did while Mark sat behind her and gently but firmly massaged all the pain away.

"Thank you, Mark. You sure do have amazing hands."

They didn't even know how they fell asleep. Both were still wearing clothes from the day before, which they took completely off and just enjoyed the nice warmth of each other's body. That's how they slept through the rest of the night. Early morning, Elli woke up and, in panic, woke up Mark.

"What is it, Elli? The twins?"

"No, no, the twins are all right. Your work. I don't want you to be late."

"Come here. I love you so much. I'll tell you something, but you need to get closer. More closer."

She was touching his side of his naked body beside hers. Mark leaned across her and whispered to the further ear, "I'm all yours today. I have day off."

Elli's body shivered a little bit.

"Are you cold?"

"I'm not. How can I be while I'm feeling your warm body heating mine?" Now she leaned gently on top of Mark and whispered to his ear, "And that, plus your voice whispering into my ear makes me react like this."

After that, Mark went on top of her and started kissing her slowly. All of a sudden, he interrupted and whispered once more, "Do you feel okay, or do you need to get some more sleep?"

"If I'll fall asleep then I probably did need have more sleep."

"Oh, it's that an explanation or excuse if it'll get too boring with me?"

"Stop it. You're something."

After that, they put all the energy that they could find into making love to each other.

Later, Elli woke up, but Mark was gone. She thought he went to the bathroom, but he wasn't there. He told her he's off the next day, so where did he go? She was curious, but the only place that crossed her mind at this point was the kitchen. She tossed the bathrobe over her shoulders and decided on the way to the kitchen to stop by at the twins' room. The door was open a little bit, which she knew she had closed. She stepped in with caution, and her heart stopped for a moment. There he was.

Mark was sitting near the cribs and watched their peacefully asleep faces.

"Hi. Here you're. I was wondering where you did go."

"Hi. Did I wake you up?"

"No. You didn't."

"Good. You need to get rest, Elli. I don't want you to spread yourself too thin, Elli. Tomorrow is another day."

"Yes. But you did mention to me you are off and all ours," Elli said quietly with a smile and gave Mark a hug from behind.

"Smart girl."

"Let's go."

"Okay. Let's go," said Mark with big yawn.

"And I think someone else needs to get more rest as well." They looked at each other and smiled.

"Are you thirsty or hungry?"

"No, I'm fine. Just nicely tired and happy and thankful. But you should at least have a drink."

"I have drink on the nightstand."

"Oh. Then we are all set."

Chapter 21

It was still dark when Mark's phone vibrated.

"Mark, phone."

"I'm sorry."

"It's okay. I was going to see the twins anyway," Elli said and slid her feet into the slippers. By that time, Mark was sitting in the bed, fully awake.

"Elli, I have to go. But I'll come back."

"What happened? Didn't you say you're off?"

"Yes. There's no change about that."

"So there is change in the part that you're all ours," said Elli with smile in her face.

"Silly. But correct on that part—but only for very short moment."

"Now I'm curious."

"Sue."

"Is she okay?" asked Elli with a voice that couldn't hide she is truly worried.

"She is … she's okay but needs to be picked up."

"I understand," Elli said, and she did. She knew Mark was the person who she needed to get help from as well; that way, once he'll help her with whatever she needs, he'll come back. And she knew as well if he won't go help her, he won't feel good about it. So it was pointless. And she saw it was not the best time to ask what it was all about. She ordered herself not to think about it and get her mind focused on something else. There was no need to think twice what that something is gonna be. She was hoping to get few minutes for herself, but she smiled and started to walk toward the twin's room.

"Hello. I'm Mark, Sue's friend."

"Sue?"

"Hey, Mark. Hi! How are you?"

"I guess I won't be wrong if I'll say at this moment that I'm better than you. Gee, Sue. What happened? What—"

"I think … I think the police officer would like to talk to you," Sue said and covered her mouth to make her hiccup more silent. "Hi."

"Hi! I let Dr. Sue Raysse call you because I know she's usually nothing like that. Thanks for coming. I know she's a good person. A great doctor as well. This will be having too big impact on her life."

"Thank you very much. You're completely right about all. She's not like that. I'll take her home, and I'll take care of her car as well."

"Hope whatever it is, she can handle it. The sooner the better. Good this time it was me and nobody got hurt."

"Thank you once more. I'm sure she'll do the same later as well, once she'll be herself again."

Both of them went silent. There was no need to say anything else. The police officer went to his car, and Mark, in silence, put the seatbelt over Sue's body. Then he drove her car to the near parking lot and went back to his car. Sue wasn't asleep. She was just resting her head with her eyes closed.

"I'm sorry, Mark."

"I know. Things happen. Overall, you're pretty lucky. I'm sure my car will be towed by this time, and I'll be sitting in the back of the police car," said Mark in a silly voice to ease the atmosphere in the car. She started to laugh and cry at once. They both knew what it was and why it was happening. That's why none of them had a need to talk about it. Mark drove them to Sue's place. He was trying to help her get situated at home, but she showed him she's capable of doing so. Since all of it happened close to her place, Mark decided to leave his car there and walk to get Sue's car to her place. Brisk walk did help him to sort his thoughts. He was thankful how Elli took the whole situation, but he didn't want to let things like this get between them.

After parking Sue's car at her place, Mark went to drop off the keys and found Sue awake and crying. He put down her keys on the tray where she used to have them. Then he walked closer to her and sat down beside her. He pulled her closer without the words and let her cry out till she went quiet.

"Sue, I'm truly sorry. I know I'm the cause of all this mess, and I should be the one to be feeling all that you're dealing with. It sucks that instead of that, I finally found what I was looking for. We were always honest and open with each other, so I can't do anything else. I can't act differently now. You're truly a great person, and you do deserve good things to be happening in your life. I wish I can do something more for you. But we both know, Sue, it won't work."

"It did. Thank you for coming and taking care of me, of the car. You know."

"That's the least I can do for you. I told you, Sue, you can always count on me."

She hid her face under his arm and let out a quiet sobbing. Mark waited till he didn't hear any sound. He knew she's asleep, so he took her to bed and pulled the cover over her body. Before he closed and locked the door behind him, he put a glass of water on the nightstand.

His body relaxed a little bit while driving back to Elli and the twins.

Chapter 22

The day went too fast. They had fun with the twins and enjoyed the time together once they went for their nap. For dinner, they set up all in the backyard and had Nick with Lisa and Katie over. The air got colder, so they all sit closer to the fire. The twins already went to sleep, so that night, they'll be the only one not smelling like it, but none of them could care less. It was a nice time that all of them will treasure as a special memory from the summer. Katie even ran inside in the house to get the phone to take the picture of them by the fire.

"I wish I took the picture even when the twins were here with us."

"Will make with them picture next time," said Lisa.

"Or I'll just add picture of them asleep."

"Katie, don't!" said Nick, but it was already too late. She was gone too fast inside the house.

"I guess we should decide who'll put the twins back to sleep," said Elli, laughing out the situation. But even if she didn't mean it, she was already getting up, but Mark sat her down gently.

"Elli, you prepared this beautiful evening. Relax now. I'll go. Who knows maybe Katie will be fast enough as well to take pictures of them without waking them up."

"Mark, pssst. Don't wake them. Aren't they cute?"

"Sorry. Yes. They are."

"They're, we're so lucky to have you in our lives. Don't wake them up. Let's go back to the fire!"

After that, Mark couldn't do anything else but follow Katie out of the room and out of the house. When the others saw them, they couldn't stop laughing about it. Little Katie just easily walked Mark out of the house.

"Twins still asleep?" asked Nick once he was able to stop laughing.

"Yes. Of course!" said Katie. "You all thought I'll wake them up?" She turned to Mark with a question: "That's why you came there? I thought you came to see the twins to enjoy them."

"I sure did, as to make sure they sleep well."

"Adults! The twins are asleep, and I do have my picture of them."

"You're the greatest, sweetie. But it's time for you to brush your teeth and go to bed as well."

"As I said. Adults!"

At that moment, all of them burst into laughter. Lisa took Katie inside.

"She's something," said Mark.

"Right! I won't change her for anything."

"You better watch out, so Lisa won't hear that." Elli was teasing Nick.

"That's the best thing. She knows, and she is saying the same."

"Hey, did I miss something?"

"Nope."

"Not at all."

"You all look so suspicious!"

"All cool. Sit down, Lisa, so we can enjoy this moment just like these two."

Chapter 23

"Lisa, hi!"

"Hi, Mark. Come in."

"Where is Elli? She didn't mention anything for today. Hope she didn't start working instead of you."

"Well, you're pretty close to reality. She had that idea few times already. You really know her very well. She'll be here soon. Hope."

"Hope? Is everything okay? She didn't sound the usual in the phone earlier today."

"Will see. Is it okay with you if I'll wait for her here as well?"

"Of course. But, Lisa, now you're really making me curious. What's Elli up to?"

"She … she'll be here soon."

"Lisa, you said three hours ago that Elli will be here soon. But she's not. You've asked to stay and wait for her here. She's not answering my calls. It's there anything I should know? Can you call her? I'm really starting to worry about her."

"Mark, will you help me give the twins a bath?"

"Lisa, what's going on?"

"Let's give bath to the twins, and I'm sure she'll be back home."

"It's already dark outside, cold. Fine, don't tell me. I'll go out look for her."

"Mark, I'm sure she'll be okay. Please, help me with the twins. If she won't come by then, I'll go look for her."

The twins were all clean and happily in their cribs, being silly when they've heard the doors opening. Lisa and Mark both looked at each other, and Mark saw Lisa was looking frozen.

"Elli? Elli?" Mark said aloud while getting up from his knees and walking out of the twins' room. He stopped by the staircase, and his eyes met Elli's eyes. She looked so hurt. So broken. In pain.

"Elli. Oh god, I'm so glad you're at home. Are you okay?"

"Lisa?"

"She's here. We just put the twins to their cribs after their bath."

"Thank you."

"Elli, hi." Lisa came out of the room as well. She walked quietly toward Elli. "Glad you're here. Mark was really hard to be hold here, not to get out to look out for you."

"Thank you."

"Hello, girls. I'm still here. Can someone tell me what's happening?"

Lisa just quietly hugged Elli, who was shaking. When they broke the hug, they looked into each other's eyes in silence, and both had tears in them.

"You're okay?"

"I'll be. One day. Thank you, Lisa."

"I think you should tell Mark," said Lisa quietly to Elli. "I'll be at home if you'll need anything."

Elli only quietly closed her eyes while doing the gesture of understanding with her head. Mark was just standing there and was trying to figure out what's happening. But he had no clue. "Elli, are you okay? I was going nuts. Lisa was just keeping quiet. Just like you now. Can you say something? You're shaking, crying. What's going on? Talk to me, Elli. Please."

Elli felt just too exhausted and very tired—too weak to talk. And she knew Mark needed to know. She needs to tell Mark what she is dealing with, but she just couldn't. Her whole body started to shake. She felt dizzy.

"Mark," she started to talk when she lost her balance, but Mark was faster, and he caught her and carried her to the sofa and wrapped her in the blankets and went for a glass of water.

He was looking at her. She looked very sad. She made attempt to start talking to Mark, but she couldn't. Mark signaled her not to talk. He got scared. He just caught her before she fell, but she was still not looking okay. Mark was looking at Elli. She didn't even know how much he loves her, and seeing her like this was tearing him apart. He wanted to know what happen. He wanted to know what he can do for her to get that sorrow out of her look. He'll do anything to change, to fix whatever is needed to be fixed. But he understood; she needed time.

Elli opened her eyes and realized she must have fallen asleep. Mark was having his arms wrapped around her. She was trying to move carefully out of his hold, but Mark just had his doctor's sleep, so he woke up right away.

"Elli, you're up."

"You too, as I see," said Elli, and Mark knew she's better by hearing her try to make the joke.

"Are you, are you okay?"

"I'll be, Mark. I just really need to go to the bathroom." "Oh, sorry." Mark realized he was still holding her.

"It's okay. I'll be right back."

Mark didn't have any idea how long was Elli already in the bathroom, but it seemed like forever. He still didn't know what's going on, but he didn't want to push her impatiently over the edge. He went to the bathroom door and knocked on them.

"Elli? Can I come in?" He knew she's not coming out anytime soon. "Elli, can I?" He put his ear closer to the door but didn't hear a thing. So he just knocked gently once more, and then he tried to open the door. He found her sitting in tears on the floor. "Sweetheart!" Mark said and rushed to her, crushed down on his knees in front of Elli. "Hey, whatever it is, it can't be so bad that we won't be able to handle!"

"Danny. I. Mark, how come I'm so lucky to have two best guys in my life?"

"Nick seems to be pretty cool to me as well," Mark said to lighten up the situation.

"Mark, I don't want you to think I'm stuck in the past. I … I love you very much. You make me very happy. You make me needful, and I hope I made you happy as well. It's just …"

"You do. Don't ever question that. I know my life is busy, difficult, but when I thought of you, the twins, when I'm with you, with you all, I feel that is exactly what I was longing for, and I truly won't change a thing."

"But for the person that Danny was, for him to be the part of the twins, please, don't take it the wrong way. Anyone can tell, by the look when they're around you, it is truly like you guys belong together. That's why I feel so blessed. I know we're short time together, and everything did happen so fast."

"Well, not for me. It took for a while to have you awake," Mark said and handed a piece of paper to Elli to blow and dry up her face. "But back to Danny."

"Yes. Today is the day when he passed away."

"Elli, why didn't you tell me? Or at least you could mention something."

"I was … I did want … I just didn't know even how I'm going to handle the things, emotions. I didn't know if I'll go to … to our previous place where I found him. Or just to his grave or places that I could remember. I'm sorry, Mark. You're very special to me in different ways. You're true original as you are."

"You too, Elli. That's for sure. I told you once, I'll make sure that even the twins will know what kind of man Danny was. I'll never try to make any of you forget about him on the purpose of jealousy or whatever other reason. You make me feel alive."

"I know. Mark, I love you very much." She started to get up slowly. Mark got up faster and took Elli by hands to give her little pull-up.

"Thanks. Come. I need to show you something."

"Okay. I'm following you." Mark put his hands on Elli's shoulders and tried his best not to step on her feet. "A box?"

"A box," Elli said while she put carefully the box on the sofa where they sit down. Then without any words, she just put the box on Mark's lap. He looked at the box. Then he looked at Elli. "May I?"

She only nodded her head for an answer. She felt dizzy; that's when she sat closer to Mark who was opening box, giving Elli a kiss on the hair.

"What? Oh my, Elli …"

She opened her eyes for a short moment and looked up at Mark. He turned back and got lost into the contents of the box. All that he could see was just Post-it notes. He figured they were written by Danny to Elli. They were put into some time order. He felt how much Elli was loved by that person, which he never met and never will. He couldn't stop reading; he realized he got so focused that from time to time, he was forgetting to breathe. From these simple notes on Post-it stickers, he felt he is getting to know Danny. He felt honored Elli shared it with him.

"Elli, sweetheart. These are true breathtaking thoughts. He probably took one Post-it to leave you a note, and he couldn't stop with one, so he added and made this beautiful treasure for you. For the twins."

"I feel the same way. That was probably the last drop after I felt like I had no strength to function without him, not for one but two kids. But we should value life to the highest. Every living thing. But the pain was just growing bigger and bigger. It was unbearable."

"I understand. Now it all makes sense." He felt Danny's love to Elli. He felt his dreams, his excitements, his hopes, his wishes, his care, his plans for the future— which he never had the chance to fulfill.

"Lisa and Nick put them somehow in time order while I was in the hospital."

"Glad they did. It's like the story in the box. The twins will be one day happy to get the chance to get through it as I did today. Elli, I feel honored for you to share it with me."

Both of them sit in silence for a while. Both of them had over and over in front of their eyes Danny's Post-it notes. He was even right about the possibility becoming a parent. He knew Elli so well. That's why he did figure out even that sooner than Elli by herself.

"Elli, after that, I don't even know how to thank you, that you named your son Mark after me."

"Mark, I didn't even think, that you and me, but when it was time to get the twins their names, I had no doubt to name him after you. It came to me so clear, naturally. Just like the name for his sister."

"Thank you, Elli."

They stayed in the same position for a while. Elli was completely exhausted, so Mark wasn't surprised she fell asleep in his arms. He could feel her heartbeat. It felt so good. It was all real, not just some imagination. Mark put the box carefully on the sofa and lifted Elli and walked toward the bed.

"I'm so sorry. I fell asleep."

"My sleepy beauty."

"You can put me down. I'm fully awake."

Mark pretended to get Elli down, but her hands just got tighter.

"I'm sure you are fully awake, but evidently, it'll be okay if I'll carry you to bed. Elli, I'm so happy it makes me want to go to the rooftop and shout to the whole world that I'm yours."

"You mean the neighborhood ... not so sure if our neighbors will be happy for you at this hour. Mark, I would like to make love to you 'cause I'm yours. Every piece of us seems like it belongs. I wish ..."

"What do you wish? Hope you'll never stop telling me your wishes."

"I wish you don't lock the door behind yourself when you'll be leaving."

"Elli, it's better to keep the house locked. You know I do like people, and this is good neighborhood, but why expose you and the kids to possibility."

"Mark, I want you to kiss me in the doorway and see you take the key from the door that we will be standing by."

"Elli ..."

"I wish you can come here anytime. No matter if we are here or not. I wanted to do this long time ago. I'm not good in not showing how I feel, especially not to you."

"Which is good."

"The key or that I'm not able to hide my feelings away from you?"

"Both."

"Oh, Mark, I was afraid to make you feel ..."

"To scare me away?"

"Yes."

"Come here, silly. My silly."

"I thought how fast all went between us, that maybe we should slow down."

"Elli, we are adults. You just mention, what I agree as well, that every piece of us is perfectly fitting, so why slow down something that feel so good, that is so beautiful?"

"So we won't burn all too soon, I guess."

"Elli, we? Look at us. Look at this life. It's already so fast, hectic, that every single moment we can save for us, it's worth it. And I won't feel guilty at all. I'm always there for others. I do deserve something back so incredibly good and real as well. So fast? Not at all to me. If my place will be bigger, I'll be asking you to take the key from it long time ago! But for myself, not even really to be there, at home, at that time, just didn't have any sense to have something bigger. I should now probably ask you, are you sure about it? Because I'm not planning to return that key ever."

By that time, they were sitting on the bed.

"And yes, you're right. You're fully awake. Me as well."

They both smiled at each other. But all of a sudden, they heard voices from the twins' room.

"I'll go. You don't move, not even your eyebrow. And try to not fall asleep."

When Mark returned, Elli made it exactly the same position, and both started to laugh, but they stopped the laughing at the same time when their hips were against each other.

Elli interrupted with a question: "The twins are okay?"

"The twins are perfectly fine, just like we do. We should thank Sue for taking the trip."

"Is she okay? Or will she be okay?"

"Yes, Elli, thank you for understanding when she called for help."

"We will thank her one day. But not now. She must have big sorrow now because of us."

"But between her and me, it'll be always something missing there in a relationship. That's why it should not continue."

"Yes. But still. It was something that she knew, and it was probably as close to good relationship as she could think in the profession which you both have."

"You're right. But she'll make it. She did understand that. So one day, we will thank her. But now, it's just you and me. Don't let anything separate us." He looked at Elli's eyes and gently pulled away her hair that was falling into her eyes—the eyes that he had to put the kiss on, on both of them, on her nose, on her neck, and at the bottom of her ear. He pulled her comfy shirt off one shoulder and kissed her on the uncovered part, and then he slowly pulled the shirt off the other shoulder; and while he gave her a kiss on that side, Elli, with her eyes closed, did quietly let out a sound of pleasure. She took her shirt off and helped take off Mark's shirt, lifting slowly from the bottom while giving him random kisses all the way up till Mark took the edge off the shirt and pulled it completely off after they both put their faces together by their foreheads for little break, after which they didn't hold back anything. At that moment, they made love to each other as there were truly only two people—Mark and Elli.

They were holding each other tight when Mark saw tears in Elli's eyes.

"Are you okay, Elli?"

"Yes, Mark. I'm sorry for the tears. These are the happiest tears ever."

"Gosh! I started to worry, that I ... you know ..."

"What? No. I don't know! But I'm glad you know I'm not mourning for someone in the past, who is taking me somehow away from you, and it's not even worth to talk about that."

"Of course. And you really have nothing to apologize for. As I said, I'll always honor Danny. I'm glad he was in your life. And I know, Elli, I can feel it. You're here with me. Completely. You made me very happy, Elli. I don't have any questions on my mind. There will be many more moments when this will hit you hard, when you might be falling apart over and over, but I want you to know, I'm here for you. Maybe I won't tell you that over and over, but you, please don't forget about that. I'm and I'll be here for you, whenever you'll need me. Don't ever think I need more. I have all in you—kids, job. We have each other." Mark went silent, but he kept looking at Elli. He took one of Elli's hands and placed it carefully into his hand.

"Thank you, Mark. Did you do that while I was in coma?"

"What?"

"Did you take my hand back then and put it in to your hand like that?"

"Yes," said Mark while trying to clear his throat. He felt like he has been caught doing something inappropriate. "Why are you asking?"

"I don't know. I just had that feeling. Felt so familiar to me."

"Hold on," said Mark while patting gently the top of Elli's hand and starting to stand up. Elli looked up at him with a little bit of surprise on her face of what is Mark up to. She saw him walk to and stop by the nightstand where his phone was lying. He typed something in before he turned to her and gave her a silly grin.

"What are you up to?"

"I thought you'll never ask."

"So?"

"So? What are we up to? I think we both need to get fresh air."

"What do you mean by that?"

"I just asked Lisa if they can watch over the twins for a little bit."

"Why?"

Instead of answering, Mark collected their clothes and sorted them out.

"Dress up and follow me," Mark said and smiled at Elli who smiled back at him. They met Lisa by the door, and Elli gave her the look with a question in her eyes: "What's this all about?" But Lisa's eyes were just saying, "I have no clue what's going on." So Elli just followed Mark out of the house, to his motorcycle, and they stopped there.

"Okay. Here's the helmet."

"What?"

"Put it on."

"Put it on? I should put the helmet on?"

"Correct."

"But, Mark ..."

"No but. I love you."

"But you won't have helmet then."

"I'll be okay. You're the most important."

"Not more than you."

"Elli. Please."

She couldn't resist even when she felt it's not okay for Mark not to wear helmet as well. She put it on her head and sat behind Mark who was already sitting on the front part looking back at her with a smile. They took slowly off, but she squeezed him by her hands wrapped tide around him.

Mark did feel her squeeze. He knew she's happy. They drove out of town and stopped at one of the closest farms that Elli was surprised they offered the ice cream. It tasted so delicious. They took the ice cream and went for walk. It was nice to walk together and indulge in ice cream on unpaved road surrounded with green color. No rush. Elli tripped a little bit, so Mark caught her hand, and they kept walking hand in hand while enjoying every moment while they were out there. She was giggling like a little girl. By the tripping over the rock, she ended up dipping her nose into the ice cream, which Mark cleared it with lots of fun. Good thing was she was so comfortable by Mark that she didn't feel any embarrassment but fun.

Before they went back to his motorcycle, they lay into the grass and looked at the sky.

It was a very pleasant evening with the sun going down. They both went quiet. Elli's face looked very distant for a moment. She let her thoughts wonder back to time when she sat with Danny on the beach.

"Elli, will you marry me?" asked Mark with a serious voice.

Elli felt paralyzed at that moment. She felt chills get down her body. All around them seemed to turn quiet. Once she turned toward Mark, he was holding the ring just made from flowers beside them. She couldn't help but smiled. But Mark smiled just a little bit. He was still waiting for her answer.

"Mark."

"Yes?"

"Hmm. Hmm." Elli cleared her throat before she continued. "You seem so serious about that for a moment. I thought you really want me to answer to you."

"I'm serious about it. You've got that right! You know me, Elli, you know I won't ever joked about that and never with you."

"Mark ..."

"Yes?"

"You need to stop that. Mark, we are together ..." Mark knew where Elli was heading with that, so he interrupted her gently to make it easier for her.

"Elli, the answer is so simple. Yes or no. If you feel it the same way as me, then you'll have no question about giving me the answer this way or the other way. So I'll ask once more, okay, and without any pressure, feel free to choose. Elli, will you marry me?"

She felt the heat. She felt his look at her. She felt happiness, safety, trust.

"Yes, Mark. I will."

All of a sudden, it seemed the cicadas let their strong voices be heard when Mark stood up and helped Elli do the same.

"Of course, I'll find the ring that will suit you better and will last longer."

"But this one is the true original." She knew she'll save it.

On the way to his motorcycle, they walked straight through the fireflies. They both were amazed how many of them did appear there. It was like walking together through the sparkles. They tried to catch some, and it looked so silly, so they started to laugh about it, and Mark happily lifted Elli and turned around. Both were happy but with a little bit of guilty feeling saying hi to Nick and Lisa when they returned. But that feeling was gone once they saw them comfortably goofing with the twins.

After they put the twins to sleep for the night, the four of them sat down to chat and celebrate their engagement.

"Lisa, it's hard to believe it—all these good things happening are real."

"I know, Elli. And to both of us at the same time! Finally, no more drama, stress."

"And how about you and Nick? I realized lately I didn't really get you much space to talk. Sorry for it. I didn't mean to be selfish."

"You're just happy. We are happy. But you're asking probably about the baby. No, I'm not pregnant. Not yet. I was tense, stress out. But I realized Nick is right. We have each other, and that is all that matters. If we'll have a little one, that will be great. If not, we should be happy and thankful for what we've got. Katie, all of you, guys."

"I'm sure, Lisa, it'll come. And you'll be a great mom. You guys are helping me so much with the twins I'm starting to feel guilty."

"What are you talking about, Elli? For that one getaway afternoon with Mark? Don't be silly! You're completely in charge of them. We're just blessed to stop by, spoiled them, messed up all, and leave it up to you to make sense out of everything, put it all back in some order."

"I guess we're all perfect fit. This way, the twins will not grow up by me as robots."

"Come on, I didn't say that."

"Ha! Yeah. You don't have to. But this way, they do have some fun in their lives as well."

"That's so easy with them. They're such funny. Two bundles of joy."

"Yes, they are."

"Okay. I'm changing the subject. That was so romantic how Mark proposed."

"I still have the ring."

"I don't see any."

"I did dry it and store it. Even the flower on it lasted!"

"I can't wait to see what and how he'll come up with the ring. Did you ask him for how long he played with that idea?"

"I didn't. But he seemed so serious even this way. The way he talked."

"That's why it's even more interesting how he came up with the idea to at least do the ring right at that spot. So original."

"That's what I told him about the ring. Exactly the same word. Original."

"I'm happy for both of you."

"Don't you think it's … it's …"

"What? Too soon? Come on, Elli. Yes, you could be dating for five years or whatever. But how your lifestyles are, I'm sure those years will be passing crazy fast. But why? When you both feel it. Doesn't that feel better than be wondering what's next?"

"Yes. That's true. He's great. I'm even able to talk to him about Danny."

"You missed him, don't you? I'm glad Mark is so understanding."

"I do miss him. And sometimes, it is so … it feels so unfair to be this happy with Mark. Each time I'm breaking, when those memories come, he comforts me. We know it'll take more time. I just don't want to push his patience too much."

"I know, Elli. But as I told you once, I don't have the feeling from Mark that he'll change his mind. I believe he's solid with all that he do. He'll do his first and last to help you, to protect you, and what's the most important, to keep you happy—and the twins as well. You can see it in his face how he cares about them. So relax and just enjoy the happiness. Don't let me remind you maybe I should say to both of us, how things in life can change. Then we can do nothing but be flexible and deal with whatever will come."

"You're right!"

"How is Dr. Sue doing?"

"Oh. I feel sad for her. Very sad. I do believe she truly cares and loves Mark."

"Yeah, it sucks. Don't you dare feel bad about it. If it won't be you, it won't be working out for them anyway. There was something missing. And you both have it together."

"But still. It feels like I took Mark away from her."

"You have to stop thinking this way. Take the reality as it is. You two are together. You both feel it as it was meant to be. Take care of what you two have. That's all that matters. We like Dr. Sue, and of course we do wish her well. Let's just hope she will meet someone who'll take away her pain and will be able to make her happy. Or should I say, let's hope she'll meet someone who she'll be happy with?" Lisa said and smiled at Elli.

"You're right. She's a nice person, so I hope there's someone like that for her but my Mark. So far, she does seem she's getting better."

"Funny that I had to be the one so logistic in this."

"You!"

They both burst into laughter that was interrupted by a phone call. It was Sue. Dr. Sue.

"Elli?"

"Dr. Sue?"

"Yes. It's me. Hi. I thought you should know that Dr. Mark was just brought to the hospital. He …"

"Is he okay?"

"He was involved in a car accident. They're running tests at this moment. But I thought you should know."

"Was he wearing the helmet?"

"Yes."

"Thanks for that. I'm on my way. Dr. Sue … thank you!"

"Sure."

Lisa couldn't hear the other side of the conversation, but from what she was able to catch and see Elli's face fading out from color, she figured out it's not the best call. But she waited patiently.

"Who was it?"

"The one we were just talking about."

"Sue?"

"Yes. Dr. Sue."

"Are you okay, Elli?"

"What?"

"Elli!" Lisa stood up as fast as she could to get lift to Elli.

"I'll get you water. Sit down."

"I ... I have to go."

"Not like that! Have a drink. What happened?"

"Mark."

"What about Mark. Elli, you're scaring me. What happened? What did she say?"

"Mark was involved in a car accident while he rode his motorcycle. They're running tests right now. He did wear a helmet. That's good, right?"

"Definitely. Let me call Nick where he's at."

"I have to go."

"I know. But I'll go with you. You're not going there alone!"

"Lisa ..."

"No Lisa. Give me a second and drink, please. You need to get the color back to yours cheeks. Otherwise, it's gonna be both of you staying in the hospital." Elli burst into tears.

"Elli, Nick will be here shortly. I'll go check on the twins.

You get ready. Okay?"

"I'm driving."

"Thank you, Lisa."

"Of course!"

"Why is this happening?"

"I don't know, Elli, but think positive! Okay? We'll get to the hospital, and we'll know more what's going on. It was nice of Dr. Sue to let you know about it."

"Yes, it was."

"Okay. I'll go see the twins."

By the time Nick got there, Lisa changed the twins and put their food together to make it easier for Nick. Elli washed her face and changed her clothes. They left once they said hi to Nick, and he got settled down. He wished them well and asked them to say hi to Mark from him. In that moment, Elli burst once more into tears. Nick's last words were just for Lisa to keep Elli calm and to drive safe. She promised to call him once she'll know what's going on with Mark.

Chapter 24

Once in the hospital, Elli felt like she can't breathe. Her heart was beating very fast—too fast. All she could think of was Mark.

"You're okay?" asked Lisa.

"Yes," Elli said and walked straight to the information desk. They're told to follow the elder lady that will show them the way.

Lisa knew she needs to stay close to Elli. She said she was okay, but she knew Elli well enough to see how she's trying her best to keep together.

Once they got to the room and thanked the lady that took them there, Elli rushed in. In a few seconds, she was beside Mark with tears filling up her eyes fast.

"Elli! Hi."

"What are you doing here? I thought we are going to have dinner at home," said Elli, trying to ease up moment.

"I thought to take you out today." Mark joined her in humor, and they smiled at each other.

"Good you're not dying. I thought I have to shake you up back to life."

"Lisa, hi," said Mark with face wrinkled from pain. "I guess we'll have dinner all three of us here. But I'm not sure if you'll enjoy it. Elli and I, we're sort of used to it." He squeezed Elli's hand by the memory of how he was sitting beside her while she was in the hospital.

"What happened, Mark? Are you in lots of pain?"

"The car was stronger than my motorcycle. The driver was busy with something, so he didn't see me. He tried to get the car in the last moment away from me, but his back side of the car took me for a short ride with him. And we ended wrapped up over the tree. The guy is okay. I just heard that." "Glad to know that! What about you?" asked Lisa.

"Hmm. Who are you?" joked Mark.

"So I guess that means you're going to be okay."

"Okay, okay, guys. Mark, what did the doctor say?"

"It looks like I was lucky. I did wear helmet."

"Which is great!"

"So my head looks okay. The only thing that we will know more later is the pain in my left leg." After he finished his talk, he squeezed Elli's hand, and she returned his squeeze.

"I hope you'll not leave me even if I will have only one leg," said Mark to Elli who just put a kiss on his lips.

"Nick is saying hello, and I'm going to call him. He's waiting with twins for the news about you."

"Tell him I'm sending 'hi' and that the motorcycle driving lesson we have to reschedule."

"What? Nick was thinking to learn how to drive on motorcycle?"

"I was joking, Lisa."

"Mark! You're lucky you're a patient here right now."

"I know. Otherwise, I won't even try to make this kind of joke."

"You're something. Nick was right. He'll have fun when I'll describe to him how you got me!" After that, Lisa walked out of the room to make a phone call to Nick.

Once Mark and Elli were alone, they smiled at each other.

"Hi."

"Hi."

"You're in great pain, aren't you?"

"Yes, sweetheart. I am. But it's really only in my leg."

"Did you hit the tree with that leg?"

"I pretty much landed on it. Good thing is the car did slid off, so I didn't have its weight on for too long, but it took me for a while to get the motorcycle off. Once I did, I went to help and pull the guy out of the car. He was getting a little bit of smoke from underneath the hood. But he's okay."

"When will the doctor know more about the leg?"

"He should be coming back later today once he'll know more. They know in the hospital that you're my fiancée, so no one should keep you away from me. I love you, Elli."

"I love you too, Mark. Of course I'll not love you less with just one leg. I just don't want you to be in pain."

"I'm okay now, Elli. Once you're here."

"Nick is saying hi, and he wishes you well. He did break into an insane laughter about the motorcycle lessons. And the doctor will be here shortly."

"Glad Nick laughed out about it. The twins are doing good?"
"Yes, they were giggling hilariously in the background."

Hearing that, Elli was very thankful that no matter what's going on, they still all hold together. All of them turned their heads toward the door when they heard the knocking. Elli realized, she's barely breathing. She saw right away on the doctor's face that it's not gonna be a good news, and from Mark's face, she felt he knew before the doctor even came back. "Hello, everyone."

"This is Dr. Myles." Mark introduced the doctor to Elli and Lisa who said in unison, "Hi."

"So, Mark, how do you feel? Any dizziness, head pain, neck pain?"

"All seems good, except the left leg. But even that got better. Now I feel pain only from the knee down."

"That is great! Unfortunately, we have to perform surgery to release the pressure. Otherwise, the fingers on your foot will be in great danger not to get enough blood all the way as needed, which you know what it can lead to. I was trying to avoid the surgery, but in this case, I did ask for consultation from Dr. Phillip. We both think it's the best chance to keep you in one piece."

"Thanks, doctor. When are you planning to perform the surgery?"

"As soon as we'll have room available, I put the team already together. You'll have the best in the team there, Mark."

"Thank you. Whenever you're ready."

After that, Dr. Myles walked out of the room, and Elli looked down at Mark.

"You knew the decision before the doctor even entered the door, didn't you?"

"Yes, it's not the pain. It's the numbness from the end of the fingers."

"I hope they'll have the surgery room as fast as possible!"

Lisa did barely hold the tears from rolling down her cheeks. She saw two people, that she was already attached to so much, facing another hard part of life but still holding together and having the hope for a good ending. She couldn't hold any longer. She let out a cry and walked to give a hug to both of them. After a few seconds when she had controlled her crying, she apologized to both of them and stepped out of the room to blow her nose.

"You're so brave, Mark."

"You're more, Elli. You didn't leave me here. You're still here by my side willing to face whatever it'll come."

"You did the same for me, Mark. You didn't know what you are going to face back then when I'll wake up. And you stayed, and you did care for me, the twins, and the other patients as well. This is just something little that I can do for you. I love you as you are. You make me happy by your personality. And if ... and if in the worst the surgery won't help ease the pressure, I'm not taking back my answer to you," Elli said and leaned to Mark to give him a kiss. "And I have one news for you as well. We're gonna have a baby." Elli just whispered gently the baby news to Mark's ear. He turned to her, and even through the great pain, he sat up and hugged Elli as tight as he could.

"Lisa doesn't know that yet?"

"No, she doesn't. I still need to go see the doctor, but the test showed yes."

"How do you feel, Elli? Maybe we should have been more careful."

"I thought it'll be good news for you," said Elli with a little confusion in her voice.

"I'm the happiest man in this moment. Having a baby with you, the woman that I love so much."

"Then what? Why did you mention that we should be more careful?"

"Just because of what you have been through."

"But you know I'm okay."

"Yes, you are. But pregnancy is exhausting for the body and I, we with the twins, we can't lose you. I'll be rather choosing not to have my own kid than put you in the risk to lose you."
"Nobody is going to lose anybody. We've got each other, and we'll get through it, okay?"

"Yes, Elli, we will. I'm sorry I didn't take the car today. I could be probably sitting with you ..."

"Mark, we don't know. Maybe it'll be worse than it is now. What happened, it happened. Don't waste your energy on it, okay?"

"Okay. Thank you for telling me now, Elli."

At that moment, Lisa did step in. She smiled at both of them. "Am I interrupting something?"

"Absolutely not," said Mark. "We just talked about the possibilities that we'll face after surgery. We took a look back to Elli and the twins' hospital days, and Elli shared the news we're expecting the baby!"

"Mark!"

"Elli?"

"Congratulations!"

"To which part of what I mention," joked Mark. Both of them turned to him and yelled, "Mark!"

"Yes. It's still not 100 percent, but it seems that we do expect a baby."

"If it's so, it couldn't be better timing!"

"Right! I told Elli I'm happy she shared the news now with me."

They got interrupted by a short knock on the door.

"Mark, it's time."

"Okay. Let's do it. Sorry. Now I should say just let's go. I'm just the patient now," Mark said and gave a little unsure smile.

"All right."

Elli and Lisa waited patiently in the hallway. It felt forever till the surgery was over. Elli seemed too quiet, so Lisa tried here and there to break down the silence.

"Seems lately, this hospital is becoming our second home. Not sure anymore where we're spending more time." This comment made Elli smile.

"Yes, that crossed my mind as well. So much happened here and seemed it just kept adding."

"I'm surprised Mark doesn't hate me by now!"

"Why he ever do that?"

"You have no idea how unpleasant I was toward him when you're lying here."

"He knew you were trying to protect me … and the twins. Thank you, Lisa. I'll never forget what you and Nick, with Katie as well, have done for us."

"I think I was even a little bit jealous of him."

"Jealous? How? What do you mean?"

"He seemed to take care of you and the twins better than me. Each time I came, he was somewhere near. The twins were having diapers changed, and when I found him by you, you were usually having a little grin, a smile on your face and not only if he was reading or telling you something but also even when I found him all wrinkled and sort of asleep in the chair beside you."

"I wish I could see that."

"See what?"

"See, how he was by me. See how you two were sort of getting into each other's hair."

"Elli, were you ever able to remember anything from that time? It seemed that from time to time, you did react on our talk or touch."

"I don't know, Lisa. I'm not sure. Sometimes I do have feelings that I do remember. But then when I'm trying to make that feeling clear, nothing is appearing. It doesn't make sense, right?"

"Don't try too hard. I can say that it seemed back then you knew we were with you. Your reactions to our talks, touch, but it's still a mystery. I was just curious. But don't force it, so you won't block it more. I guess."

"I'm trying to not to force it. But I do want to remember. It feels weird to know I was just lying there, and you all were around me doing first and last for me and the twins. Speaking of them, I should call Nick to find out how he's handling the twins."

"Yeah. Or should we say, how the twins are handling him?"

After that, they both went quiet and burst into laughter by the imagination of the twins overruling Nick. Elli had to signal to Lisa to get quiet since she already dialed Nick's number.

After she ended the call, Elli turned to Lisa.

"They're for sure having a good time. I do miss them. When will they be done with the surgery?"

"I know. Be patient. They're doing their best. Mark is one of them, Elli."

"Lisa, I'm so tired."

"How tired? Do you feel weak? Too exhausted? Do you want me to take you home?"

"No. I won't go. If Nick can be with the twins, I'm very thankful for it. And here, where I'm, it's exactly where I need to be. I can't imagine going somewhere else."

"But you know, even Mark told you so, do not push yourself too much. You can get over the edge, and nobody knows how it'll be then."

"Lisa, all I was trying to tell you is that I'm tired as sick and frustrated of these things that keep happening. We basically don't really get a break. It's one thing after another. Finally, I was getting the feeling that all is settling down. I stopped even thinking about some kind of guilty feeling toward Dr. Sue. I know. I know, which I shouldn't have in the first place."

"Good you know that! You can't be the one responsible for everything and everyone."

"I know, and I'm not trying to. Lisa, thank you for being here with me. It's all much easier."

"Of course! How do you feel?"

"I'm sure you mean my pregnancy."

"Yes. Everything is really happening so fast we didn't really have time to talk about that."

"I was hoping to hear from you—that you guys are expecting."

"Elli, it's okay. Really. We have Katie, the twins, and as you know, with Nick, I have finally good, healthy relationship. I'm happy. Yes, I did have moments when the thoughts of it got me sad, but then I just force to remind myself all, what I'm blessed with, and I'm fine. Fine, fine. Hey, there's still hope."

After that, Lisa winked at Elli, and they both smiled.

"But you didn't answer to me. How are you?"

"If, if I'm pregnant, then I'm doing great. So far, I'm full of energy. Eating is fine. So good. But I still didn't go to the doctor to get confirmation."

"Will you keep the same doctor? Will you go to Dr. Sue?"

"Good question. Tough one. I don't know, Lisa. One part of me wants that, but the other one is like suggesting to get to a different doctor. It's sort of—"

"Awkward?"

"Yes. Awkward and sort of cruel."

"Elli, cruel it'll be, if it was done on purpose to hurt her—with intention. But your relationship with Mark is nothing like that. You guys are just happy together. Just one look at you two, and it's obvious."

"Yes. We are happy. But I don't want to hurt Dr. Sue by our happiness. It just doesn't seem right. You know."

"Elli, just be happy and decide about the Dr. Sue by your instincts."

"It's hard."

"Then let it go. Don't think about it and make the decision when you'll be ready to call to make an appointment."

"That sounds good. I don't have to make that decision right now since we are where we are, still in the hallway in front of the surgery room, not knowing how it's all going inside."

"You know, I think it's good that it's taking such a long time. To me, it means that they're restoring as much as possible."

"I hope so. I hope it doesn't mean some complication prolonged the duration of the surgery."

They both were nervously walking in short distances in the hallway, both too nervous to sit down and wait but both tired and getting exhausted of the walks. They collapsed at the same time on the seats, touching the wall on the same side of the hallway. At the same moment, when they both finally sat down, the doors of the room leading to the surgery room got wide open. Elli and Lisa jumped up from their seats. Almost breathless, both were looking at the doctor that came out to inform them about the surgery. The doctor was pretty confident about the whole surgery performance. But he pointed out that the first twenty-four hours will be critical. After thanking the doctor for his great job, they both waited till the doctor was completely gone from the hallway, and they crushed their bodies back down to the seats. They sat like that for a while quietly when they looked at each other.

"What a relief," Lisa started.

"Yes and no. You've heard him. Twenty-four hours will tell us more."

"I know, Elli. But we have to take all good news that we can. So my suggestion now is to get straight home, get shower, look at the twins of course, and after eating, get some sleep. Tomorrow will be here sooner than we can imagine. Agree?"

Elli only slowly nagged her head in gesture of agreement. After getting into the car, Elli said quietly, "I just wish they let us see him."

"You know very well how it works in the hospital. And for sure, we don't want to exposed him to something. He needs all his healthy strength, just as we do. So let's get home," Lisa said and gave a tired but reassuring smile to Elli.

Elli called to the hospital while she took the twins for a stroller ride. She was told that so far with Mark, all in surgical part looked great. He's waking up and falling asleep. She was so happy after the news she felt she needed to share it. Lisa wasn't available at that time, so she called Nick. He did pick up and was very happy about how things were at the moment with Mark. He told Elli by what time he'll be approximately at home so they all can go together to see him and that if she would like to stay, they'll take the twins home and just continue their routine.

By lunchtime, Elli received a call from the hospital about a complication. She was trying to reach out to Lisa and Nick, but none of them did respond, so she left them short messages about the situation and that she was heading to the hospital with the twins.

It felt a little bit chaotic while she was trying to keep her smile for the twins while interacting with them and packing their stuff. It was all overwhelming. She felt guilty she ever left Mark alone in the hospital. She couldn't hold it anymore, and before she sat behind the steering wheel, she refreshed her face with cold water. She didn't want Mark to be in pain. But at this moment, he was. He didn't want to use the strong medication so he will be aware of what's going on with his foot fingers. She rushed to the hospital, and at the information desk, they were so nice to get someone to escort her and the twins straight to Mark's room. Elli opened the door with a little bit of shaking hands. Once the door got open and she saw Mark resting with his eyes closed, she couldn't help but let the tears out. Once again, she smiled as well while she stopped the stroller and leaned over Mark's body to get him a kiss. He opened his eyes and gave her happy but tired smile. Elli was still leaning over him, and he put his arms as tight as he could around her.

"Hi. How are you, guys? I should get dressed up. It's so boring here without you all."

"Get better, and you'll be begging to be having chances to get bored!"

"That's not gonna happen. You know it, Elli."

"Just wait. Just wait."

"Were you having a chance to go to see the doctor?"

"Yes. Yours few hours ago."

"Not mine. Yours?"

"Not yet."

"Please, make an appointment. I want you to be safe. Pregnancy takes so much energy, and I don't want you to be in danger—all alone with the twins at home."

While Mark was talking, he signaled Elli to get the twins to him. His face lit up while he was interacting with them. Unfortunately, this moment didn't last for too long. The doors got suddenly open, and they both looked at each other as teenagers caught doing something that they're not supposed to do. Elli was trying to take the twins fast from the bed and place them back to the stroller.

"Hi, Elli, Mark. How are you?" Evidently, the Dr. Myles wasn't there to have pleasant conversation with them. He started mechanically checking all Mark's vital functions and uncovered his foot. It was very hard to read his face for some answers. He had years of experiences to not let it show. After he was done, he looked at Mark.

"Another surgery?" asked Mark without waiting for the doctor to start. He only answered by signaling with his head at first.

"I'm sorry, Mark. Seems some nerve connections were interrupted for too long time."

"How much?"

"I'm not so sure yet. I hope it's one or two."

Elli kept quiet and the twins as well. They're occupied by looking around and munching on their snacks. She was so scared for Mark. She wished to be her, not Mark on the bed before the surgery.

"Mark, time is precious. The sooner the better."

"Please, give us a minute."

"Okay. One minute."

"Thank you."

The doctor quietly walked out of the door to give them privacy.

"Elli."

"I know, Mark. I'm sorry it's happening—something like this—but I want you to know this doesn't change a thing on what I feel for you. I love you as you are, yourself. You are a great person this way or that way." She gave him a kiss, and both of them were trying to hold their tears back.

"I love you too, Elli. And the twins and our baby-to-be."

"Is there any other way than surgery at this point?"

"No."

"Okay. I'll be here."

"Take the twins home."

"Mark, the twins are okay with me here, and Nick will be shortly ending his job, and then he'll be stopping by to pick them. I left him and Lisa a message where we are and before I did talk to Nick. That's how I know he'll be not at work for too long."

"Hi," said the nurse after stepping in no more than one minute later after Dr. Myles left the room. "Hi," both of them said back. "Ready?"

"Yes."

"All right. The doctor is getting ready."

All of a sudden, Elli found herself once more in the same hallway. But instead of Lisa, there were the twins with her and that understanding that this time, Mark will be different after the surgery. She didn't mind the look; she was just worried for Mark, how he'll take the reality. She couldn't even imagine losing part of the body. She felt so tired and sad. She was so thankful the twins made these thoughts disappear. But even after Nick's arrival, it was obvious she's worrying a lot about Mark. She knew he was strong. But how much? What will be his reaction after the surgery? How much can one person handle?

"Elli, hi. Thanks for the message. I came as soon as I was able to."

"Hi, Nick. I'm glad you're here. Mark ... Mark, he was in so much pain."

"So now is this final? Will he ..."

"If they won't be able to clean the infection and do reconnection, then yes."

"I'm sorry, Elli."

"I know. Me too."

Nick stepped toward Elli and gave her a hug. She was shivering. All of a sudden, she started sobbing. Nick didn't say a word. He just stood there and held her.

The twins were doing great. Even a few nurses came to see them and took them to show them to other personnel of the hospital who were involved in caring for them while they're staying in, till Nick and Lisa were able to take them home with them while Elli was the patient.

Lisa came at the moment when Elli was leaning with her forehead on Nick's chest. She knew at that point that whatever is happening, it is cruel, unfair. She felt stomach sick just to think of the possibilities.

"Hi."

"Hi," Nick answered, and Elli was hugged by Lisa at that moment too.

"I'm so scared for him."

"He's strong, Elli. He'll get through it. Trust me. And with you by his side, he'll be okay."

They all waited quietly in the hallway just to find out what the surgery will discover and what's next. The three of them knew they won't be able to see him straight after surgery. Rules. Reasonable rules.

As before, Dr. Myles stepped out and stopped by them to inform them shortly that they tried just to clear the infection and carefully revised all nerve connection. Now they have to wait to see if that was all that was supposed to get done, or they'll be in need to go for a second option. After that, the doctor let his words hanging in the air and gave them space to accept while he thanked them for waiting so patiently.

"Mark will be glad to know all of you were here after he'll wake up. I'll make sure he'll know about it. He's one lucky man." After the word *lucky,* the conversation went a little bit awkward, so the doctor just asked them to get home to get some rest. He or a hospital staff will call Elli about any changes.

It seemed that Dr. Myles disappeared in seconds from their sight. Elli wanted to wait—to just stay close by— but Nick and Lisa did a great job to talk her out of it and get her to the car. They took care of the twins first. Both were tired from all the attention at the hospital. After they were put to sleep, all of them sat down, exhausted for the meal. At one point, Elli broke down and cried, but Nick and Lisa didn't try to stop her. It was good for Elli to let it out, to feel better after. And she did. She felt lighter and exhausted enough to get some sleep. Lisa offered to be with the twins; she'll get to do her work in later hours. All was approved by her boss.

Elli went straight to bed after a quick shower. While Nick and Lisa turned on the TV for a short time, but no matter how hard they tried to focus on it, both of them fell asleep. So they just moved to their beds as well.

In the early morning hours, both woke up by the bell. Nick went downstairs to see what this was all about. Not fully awake, he opened the door where Elli was standing, all dressed up with baby monitor in her hand.

"Nick, hi."

"Elli, what's going on? Why are you all dressed up?"

"Nick. Mark."

"Did they call you from the hospital?"

"Yes," said Elli, having hard time not to burst into tears. Nick hugged her and took the monitor out of her hand.

"Come on in. I'll let Lisa know what's going on, and I'll take you to the hospital."

"No. No. You need to get some sleep. I'll be fine to drive."

"Elli, it's okay. I'll be getting up soon anyway. Lisa will be here for the twins. And I'll just go to work straight from the hospital. I'm good. Can you please make coffee for both of us till I'll talk to Lisa and get dressed up?"

"Sure. But, Nick, you really don't have to."

"I know, but I want to. Mark is my friend."

"Thank you—to both of you."

"Okay, let's keep going. You, coffee. Me, talk to Lisa and dress up."

Before Nick got downstairs, Lisa joined Elli for a cup of coffee. Nick found them in a peaceful mode. Lisa was able to put Nick's breakfast together and for Elli as well, even when she wasn't sure she'll be able to eat. While giving a hug to Nick, she told him to give his best try to get her eat some food.

"Ready?" Nick asked Elli.

She grabbed their coffees and food, and then she just moved her head in the sign for yes.

Lisa decided to get extra clothes, phone, and a book, and then went to Elli's place. She turned the monitor quieter, just in case she'll fall asleep. But she was sure once the twins will wake up, they'll let her know. And they did. She was able to get some more sleep even after coffee with Elli.

I guess it's true the caffeine in coffee will kick into our system after forty minutes with energy, thought Lisa while heading to the twins' room. So far, no text or call from Nick or Elli. The twins were so goofy, so it was impossible not to laugh. It was great to be around them.

Nick was glad he was able to make Elli eat all that Lisa packed for them and slowly indulged in their coffees. Both were tense of the unknown—what they'll face—but Nick told Elli it was not so hard on them as it was on Mark. Time was passing fast, and then they finally heard the door opened. Elli felt dizzy, but Nick saw it, and he grabbed her arm for support.

Dr. Myles just confirmed what they expected— removing two of Mark's fingers from his foot. It was clear he was upset about it as well. But they all knew it was possible to happen, and in that case, it was necessary to do it. This way, they were giving a chance to let Mark's body avoid something worse or complete tragedy. He left with the same words as before, that they can probably get to him after twenty-four hours if all will go well and no complication will happen. Nick was glad he didn't leave, so he took Elli home. He knew she'll be staying if he won't be there. This way, she just, without any words, followed him to the car. None of them let Lisa know what's going on or that they're on the way home. So when they appeared by the door, she was a little bit surprised. She saw them sad, so she tried to ease the moment by a joke that she's glad she did dress up. Otherwise, they'll be basting her in pajama. Both made sad smiles on her joke, so she knew Mark went through more complications, and she wasn't even able to finish that for herself.

Elli threw herself to Lisa's arms. Nick showed to Lisa the number of Mark's fingers removed. She closed her eyes and cried quietly. They all understood the situation, just not the unfairness in it. Just as they knew if this is it, he'll be lucky. At this moment, they faced another almost twenty-four hours to see what's next.

Nick left the girls with the twins and went to work. He said if anything, he'll be on the phone.

Later, when the twins were going for their nap and Lisa was sure Elli will take one as well, she went to work as well. It was a lot to catch up, but she knew she can handle it. She tried to tackle even most of Elli's work, since she started to work part time for the company.

By 7:30 p.m., she decided to head home. Before she got there, she talked to Nick. He was going to stay at work for another two hours if they won't call him about Mark.

Lisa felt tired but satisfied with how much she was able to tackle at work, and since Nick was still at work, Lisa went straight to Elli's. She was about to finish dinner with the twins, so she took a fast bite with them as well, and they decided to take them for a stroller ride. It was great for all of them.

Lisa started to give the twins a bath, while Elli made a quick call to the hospital. Mark was recovering well from the surgery. There were no complications at that time. She was told it'll be okay for her to come to see him after the doctor's check up in the morning.

She felt relieved when she heard that. Lisa told her all about what she was able to get done at work so she'll be able to stay with the twins while Elli will go to see Mark.

Chapter 25

Once Elli arrived at the hospital, she hurried from the car all the way to the floor where was Mark's room. But she was stopped at the first door where she was told he requested to not to let anybody in, which everyone knew it was all about not to let Elli in to see him. She was shocked, confused. That was something that she never expected to happen. She stepped aside from the desk and pulled out the cellphone to text Mark. Elli knew he has his phone near. No answer.

After sending the text, she called to Lisa. She wished to have her there. But then she'll probably be getting even through the desk lady. So she let go of that idea. Mark must have a reason to do so. She felt torn. But after thinking what to do next, she asked to talk to his doctor.

By the time he got to Elli, she blew her nose and wiped her eyes. He could tell easily by the look on her face that she was crying. With very calm voice, he was trying to make sense to Elli about Mark's reaction. He's behavior was adequate to the situation—very common. He asked Elli to be strong and not to give up.

While heading to the car, she passed Dr. Sue. She had red eyes as well. They stopped for a brief moment to exchange few sentences, both carefully avoiding saying something about Mark. Elli did promise to set appointment with Dr. Sue's office. She understood, or she was trying her best to understand what Mark was doing, but she was hurt. She felt like she was not trusted enough to be by him at this time. That was exactly the place where she was supposed to be now. She sat mad behind the steering wheel and was about to start the car when Nick called. She put her hand with the keys down.

"Elli? Hi!"

"Hi, Nick."

"Are you driving?"

"I was about to start the car when you called me."

"Are you going to be okay to drive? Otherwise, I can be there in ten minutes."

"I'll be. I'm just so mad, Nick! I wasn't able to get to see Mark!"

"I know. I just spoke with Lisa. I know it sucks, but it'll be okay."

It's just all new for Mark. Don't be mad at him. Must be hard for him already."

"I know, Nick. And I do understand that! The thing that I don't understand is why it has to be this way."

"We all are reacting in a different way."

"And Mark didn't know any better. Lucky him to be by me whenever I was in the hospital. I never shot the door for him."

"It'll be okay, Elli. Just drive safe if you're sure you don't want me to stop by and pick you up."

"Thank you, Nick. I'll drive carefully. I was mad, very upset, but now I'm okay."

"Good. Then I'll see you at home at some point today."

"Don't work too hard!"

"I'll do my best."

Elli got safely home. Lisa was full of questions. She was, as Nick and Elli, understanding of Mark's behavior but all emotional, mad as Elli for how he shot Elli out.

After dinner together, Elli asked them for a favor. She knew Katie was coming, and she was looking forward to spend time with the twins, so she said she'll try to get to see Mark again.

Lisa only told her to give a try. Later, Elli texted her from the hospital that she was there. She was observing for a while the dynamics of the hallway. She saw there were gaps of a person at the desk to pass to get to Mark's room. She knew which one it was, and she was pretty sure they didn't change it. It was already after dinner, so she knew, she had a decent time to not step into anybody. If when she'll get in, Mark won't buzz for help. She had to risk that. It didn't feel right to be like this—to be forced to stay behind the doors not to be able to see him, to be by him. She felt a little bit nauseous, but it wasn't so bad as it was with the twins.

She took a deep breath and successfully passed the front desk and the door to the hallway to Mark's room. She didn't even look around before stepping in. She felt horrible, but she didn't see it the other way at this point. She pushed the door handle down and stepped in. Mark was lying on the bed—asleep.

Her eyes quickly filled up with tears. She saw the chart with his medication. And it looked like he took the sleeping pill as well. She also saw the time for next checkup. So she sat quietly for forty minutes before the alarm, and then she texted shortly all info to Lisa and if it's okay for her to stay. She was happy for Elli to make it in. Nick thought it was insane. But then he admitted in this situation—by now he knew as well Elli is pregnant with Mark—it was so unfair to her.

Later, they sent few texts to Elli of Katie with the twins.

Elli was sitting quietly beside Mark's bed, very thankful she could see him. The room was softly lit by the exterior light, so there was no need for other lights to turn on to see him. He was fully asleep.

She looked around to decide where she'll hide when the nurse will step in when she will hear the steps stop by the door.

She turned the phone off and went fast under the other bed. The door opened. To her surprise, she recognized the voice of Dr. Raysse. She was talking quietly to Mark. Her voice was trembling she was wishing Mark didn't ever meet Elli and that it was her, Sue's fault, because she was on that stupid trip. Nothing like this will be ever happening, but that she'll do her best to protect him. By these words, Elli felt chills. Maybe it wasn't Mark at all who closed the door for Elli to come to see him. If that's so, she'll never ever go to her as her doctor!

Dr. Sue was sitting there for over an hour, and Elli felt she was getting cold. She was glad when the nurse came in for a checkup, and they both left. She knew Dr. Sue will be heading home for tonight, as she mentioned that to Mark while she thought they're alone.

After that, Elli pulled herself out underneath the spare bed and texted Lisa what she just witnessed. She was so cold, and she wanted to feel Mark close, so she just carefully lay beside him and took his hand between hers. She checked the alarm for another checkup hour. After that, she knew she needed to disappear before morning routine. By that time, Elli wished Mark will be up so she can talk to him—just for a short time. She didn't know what's going on, but it didn't feel right. And she needed to know.

After passing the last nurse visit, she checked with Lisa how they were and that she needed to stay till morning to be able to talk to Mark.

Before she knew, she fell asleep. It felt so good to feel Mark's body and to hear his breathing. She missed him so much.

She woke up a little bit disoriented but with a nice feeling like someone was touching her hair gently. And then she heard a voice softly saying her name. She saw her body covered, which she didn't remember doing so. So she panicked.

"It was me, Elli. I covered you. You were getting too cold."

She looked up at Mark's face with eyes now wide open.

Dr. Sue just arrived to Mark's room and put her hand on the door handle, but she didn't open. She thought she heard voices. "Mark!"

"Elli, I'm so happy you're here. I thought you're too busy to come to see me." His voice sounded so insecure.

"I was here for all surgeries. I was here after, but I wasn't let in."

Then she shortly mentioned Sue's visit late last night. They both went quiet.

"I thought you don't want to see me. See us."

"How could you?" He squeezed her tight. Then he gently touched her face. "Me waking up today and having you by my side. It just felt like the dream had come true."

"How do you feel?"

At that moment, Sue started taking the step back when the nurse appeared behind her. She asked her to go help her out with some morning stuff. But her head kept turning to the door of Mark's room.

"I think this was it, and there will be no more surgeries. I'm sorry I didn't stay in one piece." When Mark went quiet, he looked at his foot.

"Mark, I told you already. You're still you, which is the most important to me. Everything else is changing. We'll change as well, but till we don't lose who we are, we will be just fine.

Because this way, we will have each other.

Printed by Libri Plureos GmbH in Hamburg, Germany